1

It was high summer across southern Utah and George Houston wanted it to end. He reached Bullhead at nearly eight-thirty, not full dark, little reprieve from the cruel, persistent heat.

'It's always cooler to the north, so that's where I think I'm headed,' he replied to the query of the hotel's retainer.

'Principle's right,' the man granted. 'Like the Yellowstone, if that's far enough for you. Heard nowhere's as cold as North Montana.'

Houston handed the reins of his grullo mare to the rheumatic old-timer. He untied his saddlebags and pack roll, slid his rifle from its sheath and glanced along the main street. Despite the oppressive weather there appeared to be much activity in the town. He could see men crowding outside the single-storey law office and jail, gesturing and shouting angrily about something.

'The heat's not slowing *them* down too much,' he observed wryly.

'Posse gettin' ready to ride out,' the man replied. 'Had us a bank robbery earlier. Threw in a killin' with it. Nasty one.'

'I guess that's enough to get you stirred,' Houston replied thoughtfully.

'Yessir. There's one in jail, but three of 'em got away.' The old timer shook his head sadly. 'Chester Jarrow was a good man. They pistol-whipped him . . . bashed his head in. That's a bad way to die.'

'He worked at the bank, did he?' Houston asked.

'He owned it. Always worked late Monday, Wednesday and Friday nights. Used to go back after his supper for an hour or so. Everybody knew it.'

'And probably what got him killed,' Houston observed. 'Being habitual's always dangerous when handling money. A banker should have known that.'

'Guess so.' The man began leading the weary mare away. 'I'll tend your horse, mister. Be around back in the corral any time you want.'

Houston nodded his thanks and climbed the hotel steps to the overhanging porch. He had a mind to stay for two days, maybe three, rest up and take things easy. Right now, the Land Hotel looked just the sort of place to do that. There would be a dining room, most likely serving two vegetables with the meat, and on a real plate. A few yards to the side of the main entrance was another doorway that lead into the bar. *A little later*, he thought and walked unhurriedly into the furnished lobby.

Orville Land was short and middle-aged, with grey eyes and a big, hooked nose. A studious, enquiring man whose eyesight was shot through from reading everything and anything which came his way, usually at night and under the poorest of lights. Straight away, he picked up on the chief characteristics of George Houston; the six-foot slim build, the clothes of store-bought quality, the blue-steel .44 Navy Colt at his right thigh.

'Welcome to Bullhead. I'm Orville Land, proprietor of this establishment,' he said from behind the reception desk. 'I hope your stay will be a pleasant one, Mr. . . ?'

'Houston,' the newcomer said, dropping his traps as he took the pen to sign the register.

'You'll be passing through . . . Mr Houston?' Land asked politely.

Houston nodded. 'I'll be staying a couple of days, three at most.'

'That will be just fine . . . quite satisfactory.' Land smiled, took a key from the frame and passed it over. 'Number four up the stairs. It's clean and comfortable . . . the way I like to keep all my rooms here.'

Houston thought the man sounded like he was referring to his mussy appearance. 'I'll naturally be wanting a bath. I feel as though I've brought half the desert's dust to town with me,' he said, as though ahead of the inference.

'Bathroom's at the end of the corridor,' Land continued. 'If you want supper, I'm sure we can arrange something.'

Houston nodded. 'Thank you, but no,' he said. 'I ate earlier . . . just about everything I had left. The most corn dodgers, beans and bacon eaten by one man, ever. I could do with a drink, though.'

'The bar's right on through there.' Land indicated an archway to the bar Houston had already noticed.

Houston could hear the growl of agitated talk emanating from the room. 'Thanks. Sounds like I won't be your only customer,' he said.

Land frowned. 'This is an angry town right now. When men are that way, they're inclined to get themselves liquored up. This is as good a place as any to do it.'

'I did hear you've had your bank robbed. That and a killing,' Houston offered.

Land dropped his gaze to the register. 'Of course. Old Bones would have mentioned it. Is it of any interest to you?'

'Right now, the only thing I'm interested in is catching up on some sleep,' Houston replied.

'I recognized the name . . . *your* name, and just wondered,' Land pushed.

'Yeah, it's usually the way I prefer it. But I've already noticed you've got a law office and a jail. I expect your officers are reliable and good enough.'

Land held back for a second before answering. 'The sheriff's reliable, so's his deputy. I won't say any more than that.' He shrugged, stared tellingly back at Houston.

As Houston took the stairs, Land returned to studying the full signature in the register. George Irving Houston. Although Bullhead wasn't anywhere near one of Southern Utah's larger towns, it was well situated. It saw many a north- and south-bound traveller, a cross-section of frontier types who had scribbled their names in the hotel register. There were drifting cowpokes and preachers, women of easy virtue, a lot of them heading for the flesh-pots of Cedar City or Grand Junction. There had been drummers hawking every imaginable kind of bottled liquid remedy, a few professional gamblers and a gunman or two. But Land wasn't certain if his hotel had accommodated a well-known bounty hunter before.

There was only the one prisoner at the jailhouse. He sat on the edge of a low bunk, grunting and groaning at the pain in his throbbing head. He looked up and blinked vacantly at the tall, string-bean of a man standing in the passageway, leaning on crutches.

Sheriff Myron Games had been unable to head up the posse. According to Bullhead's physician, it would be two or three weeks before the lawman would be able to ride competently again. His left

leg was between hickory splints and he wasn't supposed to be up and about, putting weight on it. But
this was a critical situation. He was in his late forties
but right now looked older. His hair was more salt
than pepper and his sun-burned face deeply
hatched with age lines. Though temporarily inca-
pacitated, his piercing-blue eyes suggested the
sharpest, most resilient lawman Bullhead had ever
elected.

'You're havin' that joke ain't you?' the youthful
prisoner mumbled. 'Murder an' robbery? Me? Hah.
It's a bit o' fun the old sheriff gets to play when his
workin' days are nearly over. Somethin' to ease the
boredom.' The prisoner frowned, passed a hand
over his eyes. 'You made a mistake an' I don't even
know how the hell I got here. How'd it happen?'

'It's no sort of fun, Billy,' the sheriff growled. 'If
you think *that*, it could be why an' how it happened.
Chester Jarrow is dead an' there's thousands of
dollars gone from the bank safe. Those three so-
called partners of yours high-tailed it out of town
but you stayed behind an' got roostered. What part
of all that's such an entertainment, eh?'

'Honest to God, I swear I don't know what you're
talkin' about, Mr Games,' Billy Carrick replied.

Games steadied himself and dug into a pocket
for his tobacco. With unhurried efficiency he
popped a chaw of Brown Mule into his mouth,
chewed for a few agreeable moments while collecting his thoughts, before explaining to his prisoner.

10

Billy Carrick was twenty-four years of age, a well-featured young man but with a too-quick temper. His pale hair was unruly, his face sun-tanned and his eyes were brown, although temporarily blood-shot. He oozed a rank, miasma of alcohol that baffled Myron Games. Even for a hell-roarer like young Billy, committing a bank robbery and murder, then drinking yourself into a state of unconsciousness was barely credible. Yet the evidence was damning.

'Listen real careful, an' I'll tell you what I'm talkin' about,' Games said, quietly but clearly. 'Then you can give me your version.'

'It's plain loco. All of it,' Billy protested.

'Yeah, well tell me that when I've finished.' Games lifted his face as he continued authoritatively. 'You rode into town this afternoon, an' went straight to the Delano hole to start your drinkin'. Remember, all *that's* incontestable, so don't say anythin' dumb.'

'I don't deny it, but I was on my way somewhere else. I needed a swift drink . . . a dust settler.'

'I said nothin' dumb, Billy,' Games returned. 'You don't understand the meanin' of a *swift* one. I'm talkin' the amount, not the speed you tipped 'em back. The barkeep says you near drank yourself into a stupor. You stumbled into the back store-room an' collapsed against the door.'

'Yeah, I don't deny *that* either. That's all I remember, though,' Billy gasped.

11

'Hmm, lookin' at it one way, that would add up,' Games frowned. 'Another way would be actin' up when you weren't drunk at all. Leastways not that *first* time. It was a sham. I reckon you were fakin' it.'

'That would make me a pretty dumb ass.'

'Yeah, goes without sayin', Billy. The window out back of the saloon store was hangin' open, because it's how you went to meet your friends, whoever they are . . . or were. I doubt you'll be seein' 'em again. Then you busted into the bank an' got Chester Jarrow to open the safe, before you beat him to death.'

'Stupid . . . stupid. What about these friends you say I had? Where are they?'

'Don't know. But three riders were seen high-tailin' it from the north end of town shortly after. Huh, a trio of real lizard-tails. Dod Levitch is leadin' a posse after 'em. But even if *they* make it to the hills, we've got *you*. You're in the deep an' treacly, Billy, with no one to pull you out. Makes you kind of sick I guess.'

'You sayin' I murdered Mr Jarrow?' Billy asked with what sounded like genuine disbelief.

'Sure am, Billy boy. What would you do if you were me? I've even got your pistol locked in my safe. The one with your initials scratched into the butt. Dod found it beside the body. We needn't go into detail right now, but you've only got to take a close look at it, if you get my meanin'.'

12

'*My* gun . . . but I didn't . . .' Billy started to stammer.

'Oh yes you did, Billy. An' you panicked when you'd done it. Only a natural idiot would leave the killin' weapon behind. Your gang saw it an' made tracks . . . left you to face the music. You should've run with 'em. Instead you sloped back to where you'd come from . . . probably fell asleep, what with the shock an' all.'

Billy's face had drained of all colour and he now started to tremble. 'I swear to you, Mr Games, I . . . I . . .'

'Save your swearin' for the second act, Billy . . . your encore for the trial.'

'Why the hell would I want to kill Mr Jarrow? I'm no killer . . . where'd that come from? You know me.'

'Thought I did, Billy . . . thought I did. But I will give you a reason or two. You an' your family have got yourselves a mine that costs more to work than anythin' you're ever likely to dig up. So you wanted money . . . a big passel of it.'

Billy shook his head in misery. 'We pay our way, we always do. We've been tryin' to get a bank loan but so's most folk in these parts. Hell, that don't mean any o' us would kill for it.'

Games took the masticated chaw of tobacco from his mouth and inspected it for a moment. 'You an' yours aren't most folk, Billy. Jarrow said "no" to a loan an' that's a motive. As for the capability, are you forgettin' all the times I've had to arrest you? Hell, I've lost count. You get liquored up an' start a fight. It's the oldest trick in the book to blame a failin' . . . as if it's some sort of charm. You get sober an' claim you knew nothin' about it. For chris'sake there's no difference here 'cept this time you went the one step too far.'

'No, you got to listen . . .' Billy started.

'No, *you* got to listen,' Games replied. 'This is the bit that could reduce you from gettin' a rope around your neck, to the rest of your natural, breakin' rocks. Maybe the jury will believe you were drunk when you killed Jarrow. I don't know. What I do know for sure is, it was *your* gun an' he had a fistful of that shirt of yours in his hand when he died. *That's* a tad more'n circumstantial. Try claimin' you weren't up to your ears against that. You still swear you did nothin'?'

'I can remember pushin' away from the bar, headin' for the back room . . . the store-room, an' that's all,' Billy muttered. He rubbed at his aching head as he tried to get a memory working. 'I recall feelin' real weary . . . scarcely keep my eyes open. I couldn't have had that many drinks. I didn't have any money, an' ain't exactly got a line o' credit. Goddamnit, Sheriff, that's why I weren't stayin' long.'

Games stared hard at Billy, thought there was suddenly something that could have made sense. 'Glim Savotta found the body,' he explained. 'He saw the riders hazin' from town. The back door of the bank was open, an' he hollered for Dod. It was him found your gun an' part of your shirt an' came after you.'

'He arrested me while I was asleep?' Billy asked in disbelief.

'While you were out cold. There's a difference,' Games drawled. He put the tobacco quid back into the side of his mouth, before continuing. 'Blind roostered with an empty holster an' a handful of shirt-front missin'. Where'd you stash your part of the take, Billy? Was there a share? It don't seem likely you'd let the others take it all.'

'I've never had any money . . . now . . . ever. An' I know nothin' o' Mr Jarrow gettin' killed or who the men are you're talkin' about.'

'You've never been able to recall much, 'specially when you're drunk, Billy. As I've already said, that's the drunkard's excuse. It don't cut much ice any more with circuit judges.'

From the street, sounds carried through the front office and into the four-cell jail. It was the raucous shouting of angry men, rash threats and ugly promises. A lynch mob was gathering, and Myron Games wasn't surprised. But by the same token he wasn't worried, was sure the law abiders of Bullhead would never allow that final, retrograde step. Angry though they were, the town's rowdies and disrupters had always been a minority. A town was deserving of the law enforcement it got, had always been Games' explanation to its electorate.

Billy's shoulders, then his whole body shuddered in defeat. 'By the sound o' 'em out there, they're set on stretchin' my neck before then. You might as well hand me over right now.'

'The hell I will,' Games retorted. 'They know the circuit judge gets here at the end of the month. They'll cuss an' holler for a while, but that's where it'll end. You'll have your day in court, Billy, an' if you *are* guilty, hang legal after a fair trial. Twelve years I've been Bullhead's lawman, an' never yet have I had a prisoner taken from me. But just in case the lid comes off, I've got the Post brothers armed an' staked out in the office. Newt's nursin' our big Colt shotgun an' if that starts revolvin', half the town best run for cover. You want anythin'? Some food maybe?' he asked, not unkindly.

'I don't feel hungry,' Billy replied miserably. 'I could sure use a whiskey bottle, though.'

'The only liquor you're gettin', is if an' when you're offered a last supper. There's water in the jug by your bunk. Make do with that.'

Moving uncomfortably on his crutches, Games returned to the office. His rainy-day deputies who were usually stable hands, were each seated at a front window, either side of the front door. Both looked nervous, anxious about the men outside. One of them soon queried the sheriff.

'What do you think, Myron? They goin' to rush us?'

'It's not likely, Newt,' Games rasped, as he awk-wardly seated himself on the old, crusty leather-covered couch below the depleted gun rack. 'I've just been explainin' to young Billy. They'll cut a ruckus, but they won't come any closer. If you get worried, poke that cannon out of the window. That'll scatter 'em.'

'Risin' wind sure ain't makin' things any cooler,' Rex Post offered. 'We must be at the edge o' one o' them twisters.'

The warm wind was coiling in from the west. The men advancing on the jailhouse were getting their eyes and noses clogged, and it effectively scattered them. Tugging at the brims of their hats, they shifted towards the bar of the Land Hotel to con-tinue their incitement and bitter condemnation.

That again was something that Games under-stood. Chester Jarrow had been an influential business man, contributed a great deal to the town's growth and prosperity, received vociferous support from those he had helped.

2

At the Land Hotel, George Houston had lingered over his bath in warm, soapy water, and appreciated the change into fresh clothes. Now, his thoughts were for a glass or two of whiskey from a labelled bottle, then hopefully six hours of uninterrupted sleep. Walking through the lobby, Orville Land gave him a friendly nod, noted that he was still wearing his Colt revolver.

There were more than twenty locals drinking in the bar room. Some were seated at small, round tables but most were on their feet, shuffling around in animated anger and impatience. One or two glanced his way as he found a leaning space near the end of the bar counter.

'One way or another it's a hellish night for Bullhead. As if what's happened isn't enough,' someone exclaimed. 'A feral animal ... a pariah dog slinks in here an' drinks among us as though it's an equal.'

Houston was instantly trying to estimate what the man meant. Some sort of significance nipped at his vitals. He took another sip of his whiskey, noticed the mood had suddenly become more tempered. He raised his eyes to the back-bar mirror as a gap seemed to open between himself and the brawny man seated by the front door.

Cuff Marteau was the town blacksmith. He wore a leather apron, had a profuse salt-and-pepper beard below dark, deep-set eyes that were fixed directly on Houston.

An elderly little man in a tight, grey suit and matching derby, responded. 'What are you saying? What's it to do with, Cuff?' he asked.

The blacksmith lifted a ham of a fist and pointed with it. 'I never did take to anything that lived off carrion . . . low-life that lives off others. Especially the two-legged kind.'

Houston had already cursed silently to himself as he realized it was *him. Him,* the big man was talking about.

'What's this about? Who is he?' the grey suit man wanted to know.

'His name's Houseman, an' he's a goddamn bounty hunter. I was up in Goose Creek County end o' last year. Watched him deliver a corpse right to the county jail. He sat his horse until the marshal brought him the bounty money . . . signed him off like a big sack o' turnips. Yeah, I remember him.' The blacksmith scowled around towards the other men. 'You hear me, you boys? He's the kind what tags some owl hoot mile after mile until he can backshoot him for the price on his head. Some even do it for gophers an' wolves. There's Mexicans still hunt for Apaches. You reckon we want to walk an' drink beside 'em?'

The man in a suit eyed Houston curiously. 'Is that right, mister? You hunt *men* for a bounty?' he asked.

Houston took a deep in and out breath, grimaced and finished his drink. All eyes were fixed on him as he turned and set his back against the bar, made it obvious he was placing the glass from his right hand back onto the counter. 'If they're wanted by the law,' he answered clearly. 'But I take exception to being called feral. My name's Houston, and I never shot a man who wasn't facing me.'

A suspenseful silence had descended on the barroom. The blacksmith's bitter remarks and accusation were a challenge Houston had heard before. He matched stares with the big man.

'You're making it hard for me to stay quiet, but I guess that's your intention,' he said evenly. 'If I let it ride, this town's going to be a real dangerous place. Some hotheads will be calling me out on the main street, others will bypass it with a bullet from the shadows. To be left alone I'm going to have to make you eat those words, mister, and you know it.' Houston looked around him at the uncertain faces. 'So, whatever happens here, everyone remember, it was *you* forced my hand. I was quietly taking a night cap. Nothing more.'

'I'll break you in half,' the blacksmith threatened.

'You'll have to try. I see you're not wearing any sort of gun,' Houston observed. 'So, fists it is.' He started to unbuckle his gun belt, aware that Orville Land had stepped through the archway entrance.

'Cuff Marteau. What's going on?' the hotel-keeper started sharply. 'You know I don't tolerate rowdy behaviour.'

Marteau advanced on the bar, delivered a few French cuss words that related to house rules.

Houston shrugged at knowing something inevitable was about to happen and calmly dropped his gun belt on the counter. He straightened, didn't flinch as Marteau came at him in a rush.

On instinct, Charles Milford MD clutched reassuringly at his small, black bag. He was almost certain his professional service would be required in the very near future. But to him, and maybe one or two others, it was obvious that the patient would be Cuff Marteau, not the stranger.

Drawing back a big right arm, Marteau made a lumbering charge at his intended victim. Houston ducked, twisted slightly and threw up a defensive left to ward off the blow. He followed it immediately with a solid right fist low into the blacksmith's belly. Marteau grunted and recoiled a single step. Houston quickly hit him again with a sledge-hammer of a blow

21

into the side of his face. He felt the man's wiry beard against the solid set of his fisted fingers, cursed and winced at the feeling.

The onlookers gasped, and Charles Milford started to rise from his chair. Marteau shook his head and called Houston a name. With a bear-hug in mind, he took a few short steps forward, groping with his hands outstretched like a big, rearing crab.

In the blacksmith's crushing embrace, Houston realized he would have been helpless. But he also thought the man would be more used to lifting anvils and horses off the ground, than close-combat fighting with another man. He allowed himself to get within Marteau's grasp, a perfect distance, then he hit him again and again, both fists one after another. He landed more than a half-dozen violent blows to the blacksmith's big face, near closing his eyes each time his fists connected with a hard cheek bone or fleshy nose. Marteau had no time to think or reconsider his stance and Houston hit him one more time in the middle of his broad forehead. He staggered back a couple of short, heavily-laden steps then his legs buckled, and he sagged, hit the floorboards with a dull thud.

Houston let out a long, thankful breath and turned to the barkeeper. 'A pitcher of water,' he requested, gritting his teeth at the pain that shot from his knuckles up his forearm.

The barkeeper filled a glass jug and pushed it across the counter. Houston carried it to the heap of fallen Marteau, rolled him over on his back and tipped the contents into his bruised and battered face.

Marteau spluttered, cursed and regained some sense.

Houston frowned down at him and muttered his thoughts. 'Remembering you're the one on the floor, are you still thinking those things about me being a back-shooter . . . still going to shout your mouth off?'

Marteau struggled to a sitting position. He looked down, blinked at his blood-soaked beard, issued one or two French expletives. 'You carrying something in your fists?' he panted.

'Just tetchiness. Now, I'm waiting for you to admit you're mistaken.'

Marteau looked up at Houston for a long moment, garbled another curse. 'If you got enough sand to take me on, maybe you ain't such a cowardly son-of-a-bitch. Don't mean you're a saint, neither.'

Houston nodded. 'Fair enough,' he decided and looped his gun belt over his shoulder. He was going to have a word with Orville Land, but decided a second drink was more agreeable.

The barkeeper poured a generous measure of Red Turkey. 'On me,' he said. 'This is cheaper than music hall.'

A moment later, Sheriff Games, hobbled in on his crutches. He had made a slow, unwieldy trip from his office to investigate the disturbance. 'Benefit of office . . . word gets there fast,' he replied in answer to the unasked question.

'Shame you can't respond likewise, Myron.' Doc Milford offered a short, tight smile. 'Lucky it's nothing for you to fret over.' He then gave a brief explanation for the lawman. 'Cuff shot off his mouth about the stranger here. He's not such a stranger now, of course. His name's George Houston, if that means anything to you. But it's all over now.'

Two men helped the irritated sheriff into a chair, helped him rest his injured leg on another. Games grunted with a mixture of pain and impatience, then subjected Houston to a searching scrutiny. 'I have heard of you. What do you want in Bullhead? Or should I say, *who*?' he demanded.

'A little peace and quiet. Same as it was when I rode in,' Houston answered with deliberate irony. 'A couple of days rest before I move north . . . a long way north.'

'Mr Houston only arrived a short time ago, Myron,' Orville Land said. 'So he wouldn't know much about Jarrow's death, if that's what you're thinking. I can't imagine he'd want to get interested in that affair.'

For a moment, Games considered Land's apparent support for Houston. 'Well get this straight, Houston,' he growled. 'Bullhead law can handle its own problems. We don't need outside help.'

'I know, Sheriff. Like I already told Mr Land, I've no interest.'

'As for you, Myron, you should be stuck in your office chair, not gallivanting around town. Your leg needs rest,' Milford reproved.

'That's what I was doin',' Games replied. 'But a bunch of rowdies were actin' up until that wind cleared 'em from the street.'

'With most of 'em headed this way,' Milford offered without hint of humour.

The high batwings were rattling, and dust wafted through the gaps. 'Some of us could do with rain blowing our way. But this here's no bean patch,' Land said, hurrying across to close an open front window.

'I reckon we're in for a long, dry spell, with or without this wind,' Games sighed. 'But the hell of it is, there'll be few tracks left for Dod an' the boys to follow.'

'Maybe the posse's already caught up with Carrick's pards,' a local contributed.

'No, not yet,' the barkeep joined in. 'From what I heard, them three curs had too good a start. They could be half-way to Robber's Roost by now.'

By the time Houston had finished his second drink and was ready to take to his bed upstairs, Doc Milford had finished applying salve to the black-smith's face. The battered man had eventually recovered, waving away assistance as he walked slowly out into the night.

Moments later, those remaining in the bar heard the drumming of hoofs. The sound was above the soughing of the wind, and Houston, guessing it was the posse returning, decided to linger.

A group of grim-faced men, their range clothes streaked with dust, pushed their way through the batwings. They were led by a tall, slim man with a buckskin jacket and wearing a deputy's star. Houston noted the silver hat-band around a black Stetson, and a bitter scowl that marred a handsome face.

Dod Levitch raised a gloved hand to quash the torrent of excited queries. 'We followed tracks as far as Ralph Kanford's spread, an' that was it. With this goddamn wind there's no hope o' cuttin' any fresh sign till mornin',' he explained briefly.

'How many of 'em were there? Three?' Games asked.

'Yeah, but they weren't anythin' to do with Billy Carrick, you can be sure o' that. Huh, wild-goose-chase comes to mind,' Levitch growled. 'They weren't the killers.'

'So, who were they?' Games continued.

'Stan Tutts, Boy Kanford, an' Thomas Hunner,' Levitch replied, taking a few strides towards the bar. 'Don't come much tamer than that.'

Games and Milford swapped frowning glances. All things being equal, the men named by the deputy were hardly the kind to throw in with a tear-away like Billy Carrick, engage themselves in the looting of a bank and the vicious killing of a banker. Boy Kanford was the Bar K man's eldest son, and Stanley Tutt's reputable nature was beyond doubt. As well as being Ralph Kanford's ramrod, he was his brother-in-law. Thomas Hunner was Bullhead's resident preacher.

Milford sighed. 'Sure sounds like your good deputy followed the wrong tracks, Myron,' he said. The doctor's words gave lie to the irony, the paradox of what whirled around inside his head. *Got to be as guilty as hell. All of them, I'll wager*, he thought.

Dod Levitch got to within a short distance from where George Houston was standing. The barkeeper served him a tall beer and he downed a good half before turning back to Sheriff Games.

'I'll take out another posse first thing in the mornin',' he said. 'This blow won't last all night. We'll find tracks, don't worry.'

'I'm sure you will, Dod. But it's where they'll end up that worries me. Someone's already mentioned some such bolt hole,' Games rasped. 'You say Savotta didn't get much of a look at 'em, so we got no descriptions to go on.'

'He's here now, so you can hear it yourself,' Levitch said, turning to Glim Savotta. 'Tell the Sheriff, Glim. Tell him all you can remember.'

The barkeep drew another beer as Glim Savotta strode forward, wrapped a big hand about the glass and stared at the frothy-topped liquid. The

27

posse-man wiped the corner of his mouth on a shirt cuff before taking a pull.

'It was dark in the alley behind the bank, I know that. I was takin' a leak after a long ride, you know how it is,' he told Games. 'All I saw was three hombres. They mounted up real fast and went off lickety-split. I wasn't goin' to run out with nothin' more'n my dick in my hand, was I? So, I wouldn't know any of 'em again, even if I bumped into 'em in here. Sorry Sheriff, I couldn't even tell you what colour their horses were.'

'Thanks, that's a lot to go on. You'll go far in the thief-catcher business,' Games scowled as Savotta's mind went back to his beer. 'So what happened out there?' he continued, turning to his deputy.

'We found tracks o' three riders, north o' town. I figured they'd be the ones we were after. I'm sorry, Myron,' Levitch offered, 'but it's not so easy in full dark, an' I'm no trail-cutter.'

'Sure, I know that, Dod,' Games agreed. 'An' this storm don't help.'

'How about we tap the Carrick boy?' Levitch prodded. 'Give me five minutes with him. I'll tap him parts he never knew he had. He'll tell us what we want to know, goddamnit.'

'I already talked to him,' Games said. 'He says he don't remember, an' for some reason or other I believe him. He's of no use.'

'How'd you mean? By keepin' his mouth shut?'

Games shook his head. 'No. He claimed he

didn't know anythin' about the killin' or the robbery. An' Billy Carrick really ain't smart enough to make it an act.'

'Well, *I'm* just about smart enough to know it *must've* been him. Who else?' Savotta drawled. 'For chris'sakes, some of his shirt was in poor ol' Chester's hand. An' his gun was on the floor inches from the open safe. It was still covered in blood.'

For the first time, a thoughtful Levitch noted the presence of Houston. His long, considered stare began at the man's boots and moved slowly upwards.

'Not a good time to be a stranger,' he said, to no one in particular. 'Who is he?' he asked of Games.

'Name's Houston. George Houston. Do you know of him?'

'Maybe,' Levitch scowled and moved closer to Houston. 'So, I hope he's goin' to stay out o' what's none o' his business. We don't need that sort o' interest.'

Games frowned at his deputy. 'I don't see why he should get involved,' he muttered.

'Yeah, well I'm just sayin'.'

'I'll take all this as a back-country goodnight.' Houston manufactured an unsociable grin as he spoke. He turned on his heel and nodded towards Orville Land who was still eyeing him keenly.

The deputy hadn't yet finished. 'You hear me, Houston?' he called out. 'We don't want your sort around.'

Houston stopped, took a deep breath and looked back at Levitch. 'I hear you,' he replied. 'Like most of Utah probably did.'

Levitch's jaw twitched and he coloured. A few of the locals chuckled at the prospect of another confrontation.

'I really am doggone tired,' Houston continued. 'But before I take the wooden hill, let me tell you this, Mister Deputy. I rode into town not looking for work or trouble. I'm passing through, so don't push me. I'll be gone soon enough. If you were a tad smarter you'd know that you could make this bank situation sound real important, stir my curiosity. Give me something to dream about.'

Warned by Levitch's scowl of ineffective anger, the drinkers now took care to stay impassive, their faces averted.

'He's someone who don't take to bein' prodded like that, Dod,' Games said quietly. ' 'Specially with no cause.'

'Yeah? Well he's a form o' life I can't abide. Worse'n a mercenary,' Levitch muttered.

'Cuff Marteau felt that way. Had a mind to mention it too. Big mistake. Don't you go makin' the same one. If you want to know what I mean, call in at the smithy and take a look at him.'

'Houston can go to hell,' Levitch breathed.

'He probably will one day, Dod. Meantime, those special deputies of ours are liable to get restless. One of us will have to handle the night watch.'

'It won't be you, Myron,' Doc Milford said. 'You're not going back there. Not with one leg.'

'I'm not goin' to sleep. I'll go to the office,' Levitch agreed.

'OK. An' thanks. Pesky leg *is* givin' me hell,' Games accepted.

'I told you to rest up,' Milford explained as he got to his feet. 'Come on, I'll see you to the boarding house . . . make sure you get there.'

3

Fifteen minutes after the sheriff had left the hotel, Levitch and Savotta moved out into the street. They untethered their mounts at the hitching rail, swung into their saddles and slowly walked towards the jail-house.

'So far so good,' Levitch remarked just loud enough for Savotta to hear. 'What's that about an ill wind that blows nobody any good? Hah, at this rate, ol' peg leg won't be too surprised at there never bein' any tracks to follow.'

The horses nickered uneasily and Savotta spit when a large gust blew alkali up into their faces. 'What time you seein' Carrick?' he asked, squinting along the main street.

'Around midnight,' Levitch muttered. 'His favoured route's always goin' to be the back way. With three o' you on a stake-out he won't have a chance. It'll all end there.'

'Smart. Real smart,' Savotta chortled. 'You do the

thinkin', Doddy.'

Levitch made a grim smile. 'In our line o' work, a dead suspect's usually a guilty one, Glim,' he said. 'An' it saves all 'round.'

'Like I said, Doddy. You do the thinkin'.'

Back at the hotel, George Houston had moved into the lobby. He was headed for the stairs when Orville Land made his request.

'Before you put the light out, could we talk awhile?' he asked. 'I know you can't be feeling like it, but if you could spare a moment?'

Houston paused to frown at the hotelkeeper. 'If you want to ask me to move on for bringing your establishment into disrepute, it was the blacksmith's fault, not mine. Blame him.'

'I do, Mr Houston. That's not what concerns me,' Land said. 'And there was no damage done, except to his face. No. It's about something entirely different.'

'Well, I know there's one hell of a conspiracy to stop me getting to my bed. And that concerns *me.* You might as well come on up.'

In his room, Houston tossed his hat onto the bed and looped his gun belt on the bedpost. He moved to the open window and sat on the ledge where he could see the nearest stretch of lamp-lit main street. The shadowy group of people he took notice of were those still milling in the area opposite the jailhouse. He saw Levitch and Savotta ride up, Levitch dismount and Savotta ride on.

The hotelkeeper had seated himself in the single rocker, and started to explain. 'I said it was something different, well it is . . . a lot different. I'm working on a book . . . writing it, that is. My folks used to say I had something storybook about me . . . a literary twist. Right from knee-high, I just took to the printed page.' At the expression on Houston's face, Land stopped for a moment before continuing. 'Sorry, I'm digressing,' he said. 'It's mainly a collection of biographies. Stories for which I've collected material over the past five years.'

'That's interesting. I guess you're well placed in this neck of the woods.'

Land looked as though he didn't fully understand Houston's remark . . . mistakenly thought there might be a sarcastic note. 'Yes, well it's not always this quiet,' he replied, with an understanding smile. 'It probably won't take the world by storm. No threat to Poe or Hawthorne. But I am making the effort.'

'I'm sure you are,' Houston said. 'Five years? What's that got to do with me?'

Land placed one small, smooth hand on each of his kneecaps and started. 'Five years ago, I was running a bar in Colorado Springs. It was pretty wild and wide open, and I was providing tables for the likes of Cody and Hickock. At the time, or soon after, there was an enthusiastic market for their somewhat embroidered lifestyles. I got to thinking there might just be a similar interest in the truth. You know, more historical than fanciful. So I started talking to them . . . interviews.'

'I'll wager you got bigger lies from *them* than from neutral observers. But I asked what's it got to do with me? I didn't know either of them,' Houston said.

'Did anyone? I actually started to put pen to paper seriously with the appearance of Roy Bean . . . him and his retinue. Before he took retirement, he was our circuit judge. Not much clemency given there, I can tell you. Some of the stories which came from his makeshift courtroom had to be de-winded for print. No one would have believed the truth. It wasn't so much the wildness of it . . . more the unbalanced punishments. Too much even for a Buntline dime novel.'

'And this is where I come in?' Houston put to the hotel proprietor with obvious incredulity.

'No. I would be talking with you in the chapter about chasing outlaws and those with prices on their heads. The theme, if I can create one, is about working with the law. I'll be trying to describe some sort of balance between those who worked for and *inside* of it, and those who worked against and *outside* of it.'

Houston nodded. 'OK. I think I understand. So, which side would I be on?'

'*Inside*, of course. I heard you say that's the way you undertook work. But that's the interest . . . the

35

siding of a rumour. Most folk, and that includes the law, seem to dislike and distrust . . .'

'My sort,' Houston interrupted.

'Your word, Mr Houston, not mine. Maybe facts . . . answers to one or two questions could be one way of setting the record straight. What do you say?'

'Yeah, well I don't *have* to answer. If I don't like the way it's going, I'll put a bullet in you.'

'You shouldn't shoot the scribe Mr Houston. Not if it's an accurate portrayal. Otherwise exactly. It'll prove a point, either way.'

'What else is in it for me?' Houston asked. 'Everything's got its price, and if it's now, I'm paying a high one.'

'A bottle of Red Turkey. Two Bottles of Red Turkey.'

Houston nodded, turned his full attention to Land. 'Start asking your questions,' he said.

'Right, thank you. Well, how . . . when did you decide on bounty hunting as a way to make a living?'

'I'm only answering for me, you understand? Most other bounty men I've crossed paths with are unscrupulous scum. If you write most of them are *that*, making dollars no matter how, you wouldn't be too far from the truth.'

'But you don't place yourself in that category,' Land offered. 'How about your motives? Are they that different . . . personal?'

'Not any more, no. Nobody ever asked me that

before, so I never really thought too much about it. Most places I go, they hear your name and think they know all about you. Usually they sidle off as though you're carrying the cow pox.'

'Yes, I saw something like that earlier. Please continue.'

'My pa was a lawman. Sheriff of Paymore County for seven years. Then Smallfield for five. When I was fifteen, I was riding with posses to hunt down all sorts of owl hoots. I learned from him.'

'Not collecting bounties though,' Land observed. 'You wanted to be a sheriff like him?'

'Yeah, he was big in all ways to me. Like a pa should be, I suppose. Only ever got beat by regulations. We'd chase some bad ass all the way to the county line, sometimes the State border, and then have to turn back. Pa said he wasn't allowed to do the job he was paid for.'

'I'm listening, and I understand,' Land said with obvious empathy. 'With the impatience of youth, you wanted to buck rules and regulations.'

'Yeah, sort of. I would have ridden on. . . trailed the bad ones across two States if I'd had to. The worth of a job half-done is nothing, was something else he said.'

'Your pa's work ethic is commendable. What happened to him?'

'He was west of the Green River, hunting down a couple of killers. They holed up in some cut-bank, waited for him to ride past, then rode out and shot him. Simple really.'

'You went after them?'

'With a full posse. We chased them all the way to Lake Powell and the county line. The posse was led by a deputy who told us it was as far as we could go. No jurisdiction, *he* said. Like hell, *I* said. It was my Pa. I trailed them to Rainbow Bridge, but they'd been and gone. The marshal suggested I go home . . . said it was his responsibility.'

'And was it?' Land asked, his interest stirred and genuine.

'Yeah, it was, but only as long as they remained in the territory. I think that's what most of the law wanted . . . what they hoped for. An unloading of their problem.'

'What did you do? As if I couldn't guess.'

'Presented him with my star. I bought a fresh horse and rode into Arizona.'

'You caught up with them?'

'Yeah. In a big cow-pen of a town, twenty miles south of the border. They treed the marshal . . . made him a prisoner in his own jail.'

'And the men you were looking for?'

'They weren't coming to me, so I had to go to them. I knew they wouldn't surrender and they didn't. I ended up with one bullet singeing my neck and another in my arm.' Houston grimaced at the memory, curled his hand around the upper part of his left arm. 'But it's a keepsake of sorts . . . reminds me to be cautious.'

'And them?'

'They both died. I became Mr Paladin, a town hero. They patched me up while the marshal discovered the sons-of-bitches were wanted in three States. There was a five hundred dollar bounty on each of them. That's the moment a new line of business beckoned.'

'You were OK with taking the money?'

'Why the hell not? I did what I set out to do . . . getting even for my Pa. I earned it. I realized that was the way to inflict reprisal *and* make a living, not sit around hoping anyone would wait for an invitation to trial. No. If they wanted it that way, I'd go after them. Stay with them no matter how far or how long it took.'

'What's the longest distance you've pursued someone?' Land asked.

'About seven hundred miles. From Ogden to Sacramento. The man was a lone wolf who robbed the Flyer and most of its passengers . . . killed one of them. That was a contract the Union Pacific paid me a lot for.'

Land appeared satisfied with what Houston had offered. 'I am grateful,' he acknowledged, rising from the chair. 'Extremely grateful. You've given me a considerable amount of material . . . fresh impetus to create something worthwhile. Can I use it all?'

'If you think it's useable, help yourself,' Houston granted. 'But get my name right and remember, I'm only answerable for me.'

'Certainly. One last thing,' Land pushed. 'The way it looks to me, and perhaps many others, a bounty hunter is more or less a social outcast. Do you think that sort of isolation has affected you?'

'You'd have to ask the many others that. *I'd* say not much. The difference between me and an elected law is a metal badge and an office. If those you're talking about see me as a pariah, that's their problem, not mine. Besides, over the years I have made a friend or two. There was once a sheriff who shook my hand for helping him.' Houston gave Land a thoughtful look. 'But why can't all this wait? Why tonight?' he added.

'Two reasons. I thought there was a good chance that, come first light, you might for one reason or another, leave town. I'd miss the opportunity.'

'Hmm. What's the other reason?'

'The one I've just thought of. If you sleep on what you've already told me, you might get reminded of something else.'

'You mean the spread-eagle stuff? The sort that Wild Bill Hickock gave you?'

'No. You look and sound too bright for that sort of hogwash. Besides, there wouldn't be any point. So you're not trailing anybody right now?'

'Hah, I wondered if you'd get around to that.' Houston looked down at his boots as though he wanted to remove them. 'The moment I leave here I'm heading north, and now it's with a brace of Red Turkey.'

'Absolutely. And our local murder doesn't interest you?'

'Not at the moment. Like I keep saying, for chris'sake.' Houston gave a weary smile, held out both hands as if to usher Land from the room. 'That was your last question and my last answer. This is goodnight.'

A minute later, Houston did remove his boots. He lifted his gun belt off the bedpost, sprawled on the bed and covered himself with a thin, single sheet. Able to distance himself from the anger and nervousness affecting Bullhead, sleep claimed him almost immediately.

4

At ten minutes to midnight the main street still had plenty of movement. Local men were patronising anywhere that purveyed alcohol, were still discussing the looting of the bank, the murder of Chester Jarrow, and the locking up of Billy Carrick. A few of them continued to loiter in groups along the main street.

From the law office, two guards looked out anxiously from cover. A front window had been eased up and, heeding Myron Games' advice, Newt Post was resting the barrel of his big shotgun on the window ledge.

'Hey, Dod. You reckon they'll hang around all night? They sure sound an ugly bunch,' he said quite loudly.

Dod Levitch rose from the couch, adjusted his Stetson, and grinned disdainfully. 'They're talkin'

big, just like Myron said they would,' he replied.
'An' they will think twice before takin' on that
cannon o' yours. Keep sharp anyway. One o' 'em
might have more muck than brain. Meantime, I'm
goin' to have a few words with our jailbird.'

'Myron's already tried. You think you can make
him confess?' Rex Post asked.

'Yeah, I think. There's more ways than one to
skin a goddamn cat.' Levitch unlocked the cell
door and moved in, slammed it shut behind him
and stepped up to the first of the four cells.

Billy Carrick was standing in the middle of the
floor. In the gloom of the candle-light, he was
staring straight back at him, appeared to be mum-
bling to himself.

Levitch wondered how long he'd been there
almost motionless, watching and waiting.

'I've been drunk before,' Carrick grizzled. 'Had
sore heads too. But I never felt like this. My head
feels like it's goin' to bust open.'

'That's why they call it pop skull in the places you
choose to drink.'

'No. There's somethin' else goin' on, I know it. It
don't feel right.'

'Whatever it's like, Carrick, it's goin' to get
worse.' Levitch leaned against the bars, grinned
maliciously. 'When the hangman slips that noose
over your head, I've heard tell it's the worst pain
ever, an' without even tightenin' the knot.'

Carrick closed his dark eyes for a moment. 'You

got nothin' else to do? Sheriff's not here an' you're takin' advantage o' someone behind bars. Is that it, Deputy?'

'You could say that. But Games not bein' here's got nothin' to do with it.'

'I'll tell you what I told *him*,' Carrick said. 'I'm no killer. Never have been, never will be.'

'It was *me* found your gun at the bank . . . part o' your shirt in the clutch o' Jarrow's fingers,' Levitch sneered. 'That jury's goin' to reach a guilty verdict without havin' to leave the courtroom. Huh, just lookin' at you makes me want to puke.'

With that, Levitch turned his back on the prisoner, propped his shoulders against the bars of the cell door.

Carrick didn't move, let his gaze drop to the deputy's Colt which protruded from the flap of his buckskin coat. He swallowed, nervously, licked his dry lips and tried to think fast.

Levitch went on goading, making unpleasantries. Without turning or taking a glance over his shoulder, he was hoping for Carrick to make his move. 'You're finished, Carrick. Why don't you tell me about those three bad asses you threw in with? Where are they headed? Where'd you stash your share o' the takin's?' he demanded.

Carrick didn't answer. He was already moving, quickly but silently forward to the cell door. Both his hands were trembling, and the top half of his head was cramping with pain as he grabbed for the deputy's handgun. It lifted from the high-belted holster smoothly, and Levitch let out a groan of realization.

There followed an unmistakeable sharp click as Carrick drew back the hammer. 'Hell, Levitch, you got me so nervous an' shaky, I'm likely to pull this trigger an' blow your belly out from your back,' he threatened. 'No sound, please, an' keep very still.'

'Is that how you shot Chester Jarrow ... an unarmed man, sneaky like?'

'An' shut it, too. Turn around.'

Levitch did as he was told, glared at Carrick. 'Whatever the hell you're up to, you won't get away with it,' he said grimly.

'I'm half-way there right now. You've got the keys on you, unlock this door. Remember this nervy finger o' mine on the trigger.'

The cell door swung open, but, for a moment the released prisoner hesitated. If he had been in a mood for nuance, he would have noticed that Levitch wasn't quite as taken aback as he might have been. Not exactly supportive, an edge was missing to his response.

Carrick stepped out of the cell. With a resigned curse and as much force as he could create, he struck up to the side of Levitch's head with the Colt. The man's jaw warped, and his mouth opened but there was no sound. His legs buckled, and Carrick caught him. 'That's for not wantin' to believe me,' he muttered, lowering him carefully to the stone-flagged floor.

He was panting heavily, his whole body nervy as he picked up the key ring and hurried to the iron-strapped door at the rear of the short corridor. He lifted the floor bolt and tried keys in the lock. The third fitted and he turned it cautiously, pushed the door open a couple of inches and stopped. A gut feeling suddenly clicked in that something was wrong, a sense of mortal danger drawing him back.

Carefully he pulled the heavy door to again. Sweat beaded across his forehead and trickled down his face. His heart was thumping wildly. *It's not right*, he sensed. *There's someone out there in the shadows, I can feel 'em . . . just waitin' for me.* With his mind racing, he retreated to where Levitch lay. He wondered about going back, using the advantage of knowing they were there, to shoot it out. *But I'll die*, he thought. *Yeah, then it wouldn't matter if I hadn't robbed a bank and killed somebody. Wouldn't matter about being innocent.*

During the moments of fearful tension, Carrick's instincts became acute, sharper than the pains in his head bones. In desperation another thought struck him and he cursed forcefully.

'Hell, if I was you, it might work,' he muttered. He hauled Levitch into the cell, unstrapped the gun belt and buckled it around his own hips. He was of similar build to the deputy, and the black

Stetson fitted his head perfectly. His torn shirt was a problem, but he didn't have time. 'I'll take his goddamn fancy coat,' he muttered.

Cursing low and profusely, he donned the buckskin and pulled down the brim of the Stetson. He loosed the handcuffs from the man's pants belt and secured his wrists behind his back. 'Shout as much as you like when you come to, Deputy, I'll be well gone. You won't even have a horse to give chase, you son-of-a-bitch,' he said quietly.

Carrick dragged Levitch half onto the bunk, backed off to the corridor and shut the cell door.

Convincing himself that the Post brothers wouldn't shoot except in panic, he walked unhurriedly to the inner door that led to the office. When he walked through, Rex Post glanced over his shoulder. He had guessed correctly that stable hands acting as guards – even though well-armed – would be more worried about hostiles in the street, than a banged-up prisoner. With his head bowed he continued slow and determined to the street door.

As he twisted the knob, Post spoke again. 'Goin' to calm 'em down, eh, Dod? Well, don't forget to pick up a quart of gut warmer.'

Carrick grunted an acceptance and tugged at the brim of his hat. He took a short intake of breath and opened the street door, stepped to the boardwalk and drew the door shut behind him. On the opposite sidewalk a group of locals nodded and

47

called a greeting. He turned away from the light of the twin-sconce lamps outside of the office, lifted a hand in a casual salute and descended the steps to the street.

At the hitchrail, Levitch's blood bay mare puffed eagerly as Carrick unlooped its rein and hauled himself up into the saddle. He swung in a half circle and started to walk past the mill of townsmen, pulling up his bandanna and pointing ahead as if it meant something they would understood. It seemed to work, and he rode on past darkened, false-fronted buildings. The street was a mix of small businesses, the occasional high-lit saloon or nose-bag restaurant, a couple of boarding-houses. He glanced furtively at Delano's Saloon, which up until now had been his own favoured dog-hole. Not until he had passed Chinatown and the downwind corrals on the town's outskirts did Carrick urge the mare to a gallop. The animal responded willingly, took the south-west trail towards the mountains and the Nevada border.

In the night shadows of the alley alongside the jail-house yard, three men hunkered side by side, peering through breaks in the paling fence.

'It's well after midnight,' Glim Savotta muttered. 'He should be out here by now. What the hell's goin' on? He didn't come my way. You two sure you ain't missed him?'

'We're sure. This has got to be Dod's doin',' Jack

Carboys suggested.

'Yeah,' Fats Denvy growled. 'When he says midnight, he means it.'

'So how long does midnight last?' Carboys asked.

'Another ten minutes.'

'Right. I hope he knows what he's doin'.'

The trio waited another fifteen minutes, the limit of Savotta's patience. 'This is a goddamn botcher,' he rasped, stretching his legs. 'You two stay here. I'm goin' round front to see what's up.'

'You do that, Glim. It'll look natural enough . . . you stoppin' by to say howdy in the middle of the night,' Denvy offered tartly. 'Don't want to look like it's an assault,' Savotta said, handing his rifle to Carboys. He walked to the corner and turned into the alley that ran alongside the jail. Entering the main street, he stepped up to the porch of the law office.

Rex Post answered his knock. He gave a narrow opening to the street door, nodding recognition he stepped back and let Savotta in.

'Evenin', Glim, or should it be mornin',' he said. 'You come to see Dod?'

'Yeah, that's it,' Savotta replied. He glanced about the office. 'Where is he?'

'He rode out a while back. I think he was concerned about them out front.'

'An' ought to be back soon,' Post's brother Rex, put in. 'He's fetchin' us a bottle . . . some fixin's maybe.'

'What the hell's that?' Savotta asked. From beyond the closed door to the cells, they heard scrabbling sounds and a muffled curse.

'Carrick.' Rex Post looked from Savotta to Newt. 'What's he up to?'

'Take a look an' find out,' Savotta said.

Newt Post laid his big shotgun across the sheriff's desk and took Myron Games' keys from the drawer. He unlocked the inner door. Savotta and Rex Post followed him into the cells.

Dod Levitch had rolled off the bunk. He was working his face muscles, trying to move himself across the stone floor with his cuffed hands.

'Christ, it's Dod,' Rex Post yelled.

'He rode out. We saw him,' his brother said.

'Not *him* you didn't,' Savotta differed. 'Use your keys, goddamnit.'

Levitch grimaced in pain. 'He must have broke my face half open. Cracked a bone or two,' he groaned.

'Who?' Rex Post asked pointlessly as he removed the handcuffs.

'Carrick, you fool. He grabbed my gun an' hit me with it.'

Newt Post looked around the darkness of the cell. 'That ain't all, Dod. He walked right past us an' out the front door.'

'You let him? You let him walk from here to the front door?'

'He was wearin' your hat an' coat. We weren't

50

expectin' anyone else but you.'

'An' he's lit out on your horse,' Rex Post muttered.

'Yeah, well he would, wouldn't he? Did you look to see which way he went?' Levitch demanded angrily and painfully.

'South. An' he didn't look like he was in much o' a hurry. I didn't know what he was up to. Now I know, an' that mare o' yours has got a real turn o' foot.'

'Yeah, the son-of-a-bitch knew that much.' Levitch made a grab for Rex Post, used him to haul himself upright. 'Kick the door o' the livery stable in if you have to,' he snapped. 'But I want a rimrock here an' ready to ride in five minutes. Glim, are your boys in town?'

Savotta nodded. 'I know where to find two of 'em.'

'Good. I don't want a big posse this time. Four o' us is enough.'

Levitch took a spare gun belt and Colt from a deep, side desk drawer and strapped them on. He lifted a flat bottle of physic, considered it for a moment then pushed it into his pants pocket.

'Myron will have to know,' he said to Newt Post. 'Go wake him an' tell him what you know. Tell him I'm ridin' after Carrick.'

Savotta went to the door and shut it after Post, turned to frown at the deputy. 'What the hell happened here?' he wanted to know. 'We were waitin' out back, just like we agreed . . . like you told us.'

'How could I have guessed he'd escape through the *front* door?' Levitch fumed. 'Hell, I even warned him the street was full o' towners wantin' to stretch his neck.'

'He ain't the dumb ass you got him figured for,' Savotta rasped.

'Just enough to head for home.'

'How'd you mean?'

'Headed south could mean Lake Mead . . . the Black Mountains,' Levitch replied. 'He'll need a fresh horse, an' who else would he go to for help other than kin?'

'He ain't got that long a start,' Savotta said. 'We could be on his back before sun up.'

'Could if we were goddamn hootie owls. Go get your boys,' Levitch directed impatiently. 'Soon, I'm goin' to feed Carrick to our Chinatown hogs.'

A quarter-hour later, the four men were hammering out of town on the trail of their quarry. There was a gibbous moon casting thin light over the desolate tract of land.

The storm had drifted away, and, after the first four or five miles, they cut the bay mare's sign. Levitch recognized the imprint, cursing in frustration, signalled for the others to draw rein.

'He knows the territory . . . turned west,' he muttered. 'You know what that means?'

'More or less. He's headed for the plateau. Shorter route to the lake,' Fats Denvy answered.

'Yeah, if you want to die. My water bottle must have been damn near empty,' Levitch said. 'Even if he refills at any o' the creeks, he won't get across that wasteland.'

5

The four riders chased the bay's tracks to the headwaters of the Colorado River. Reaching a narrow, fast-flowing creek, they found evidence that their prey had paused to fill Levitch's canteen. In the soft ground above the sloping bankside were the clear impressions made by Billy Carrick.

'It's where they took a drink,' Denvy said.

Savotta looked to where, beyond the creek, the bay's tracks continued. 'Dod, I really don't want to chase him into that godforsaken place. That weren't in the deal.'

Levitch swallowed, thumbed down the cork in his bottle of physic. 'We'll follow his sign till we know for sure that's the way he's gone,' he replied.

In the early hours of the morning, they topped a low rise and reined in. Stretching west was the vast expanse of scorched, barren land known as Tierra Sin Vida – mile after mile of miserable country that, over the years, had claimed many an unsuspecting soul. Even tough prospectors who had ventured into its emptiness, disappeared, never to be heard of again.

'He's got my blood bay, but he certainly didn't leave the jailhouse with anythin' more'n the spit in his chops,' Levitch said.

'But it's still a short cut if he's headed home,' Jack Carboys held.

'A canteen won't last him. Even a full one,' Denvy added.

Levitch grunted with aggravation. 'For chris'sakes, is he headed home or not?' he challenged.

'Won't pay to be too over-hasty,' Denvy shrugged. 'Let's think about why he's goin' that way. If it's home he's headed for, what next?'

'Just say what you're thinkin', Fats. Same goes for all o' us,' Levitch offered.

'If he does make it home, he'll be a dead man ridin'. If he can talk, he'll make sure his kin know what happened. Whatever you think of Billy Carrick, his family are square-dealers . . . all of 'em,' Denvy looked to Levitch who nodded for him to continue.

'Real likely, his pa will get suspicious when he hears about how the jail break went. He might even take a close look at that Colt of yours . . . see those pinchbeck cartridges in your gun belt.'

'And? What could they do about it?' Levitch asked.

'Probably get angry an' head straight for town to

meet with the law,' Denvy continued at a pace. 'But not you, Dod. They'll pass you up an' make their case to the sheriff.'

'Fats is right,' Savotta said. 'Maybe there ain't much chance of the kid gettin' clear across this desert. But what if he does, eh, Dod? What if he does?'

Levitch stared out west across the moonlit landscape then to the south. 'The likely trail to the lake is a longer route,' he said, 'but Carrick's goin' to be at walkin' pace. If he makes it at all, you'll be well ahead o' him,' he added grimly.

'How much time should we give him?' Jack Carboys asked.

'Three days at most. If he's not out o' that hell hole by then, he never will be.'

They descended from the rise, rode another hundred yards, still following the sign left by the bay. Levitch dismounted and picked up his buckskin jacket, dusted it off and stowed it in his saddle-bag.

'Son-of-a-bitch don't know worth when he sees it,' he muttered derisively.

'He kept your pretty bonnet, Dod,' Savotta jested. 'At least he knows the price of silver. Besides, come tomorrow, that desert sun will be hotter'n hell's kitchen.'

'Well, I guess that's it,' Levitch decided as he remounted. 'Glim an' Jack take the long trail. Fats an' me are headed back to town.'

'You figure Games will be satisfied with all this?' Savotta asked.

Levitch nodded. 'Yeah, if it suits. Why make a fuss? He can report Billy Carrick broke jail 'cause he'd earned a rope. An' when he rode off he was signin' his own death warrant.' The deputy grinned wryly. 'Ol' Myron can wire all the peace officers from here to kingdom-come to be on the look-out for three strangers.'

'Yeah, very specific,' Carboys sniggered. Savotta and Denvy swapped complacent grins.

'So, it's Amen.' Denvy gave a snorting laugh. 'See you in a few days, Glim.'

'Let's move out,' Levitch ordered.

Levitch and Denvy swung their mounts away, and began their return journey to Bullhead. Carboys and Savotta rode south towards the regular trail that linked the State border with Lake Mead.

For the first mile or so, Levitch and Denvy travelled in silence. 'About that jimson you fed young Carrick,' the deputy asked eventually. 'How long will it last?'

'For his head to clear? About now. The Apache can make it last for three days. But that's when they're takin' on the US Army.' Denvy grinned. 'Not that a clear head's goin' to help him where he's set for.'

'His mind was sharp enough when he clocked me,' Levitch growled. 'I expected somethin' o' the sort, but I never thought he'd steal my hat an' coat.

Huh, more front than the Alhambra. Someone else might admire that.'

'Yeah, they sure might, Dod,' Denvy grinned wryly again.

Levitch shook his head in puzzlement. 'Why in hell didn't he sneak out back? It was the natural thing for him to do . . . for anybody to do.'

'Maybe he checked your Colt an' found out they were quack bullets. Maybe he didn't like the look of it,' Denvy suggested.

'Sounds like you're enjoyin' this, Fats,' Levitch grated. 'No, Carrick didn't have time for anythin' like that, goddamnit. He made up his mind, quick like.'

'He knew somethin' was up,' Denvy said. 'Funny thing is, while we were staked along that fence, I thought that rear jailhouse door opened. The light sort of changed. I thought it was my eyes playin' tricks in the dark. I guess we'll never know.'

'No, I guess not,' Levitch grimly agreed. 'But if by some miracle he *does* reach the west end o' the desert, Glim and Jack will be waitin' for him.'

'Waitin' for his body, an' your hat.' Denvy chuckled softly. 'I just thought of somethin' else funny, Dod.'

'Yeah, what's that?'

'If he comes up against Jack an' Glim, maybe Carrick will have enough life in him to try firin' your Colt. That'll be mighty funny, goin' for a shootout with duff beans in his wheel.'

'Yeah, mighty funny. I'm almost laughin' myself from the saddle.' There was silence for a few moments before Levitch continued. 'It could be there's somethin' wrong with you, Fats,' he said. 'Bein' a murderin' bank robber's one thing. Carrick's another. He's nothin' more than our fall guy an' you know it. He's just servin' a purpose. Hell o' a thing, but that's the way it is.'

At first light, Levitch met with Myron Games at the Widow Book's boarding-house. Games had taken a few deep breaths at the news of the escape. With hardly-suppressed anger he reprimanded the deputy for negligence, slowly conceded as he calmed himself down.

'It sure gives meanin' to love thine enemy,' he said. 'I'm not sure how much we can learn from this, Dod, other than don't put guns in their hands.'

'It could be worse,' Levitch tentatively suggested. 'As far as I'm concerned, there was never any doubt o' Carrick's guilt. Now he's proved it by ridin' into the Tierra Sin Vida.'

'Yeah, if that's where he's gone. He probably knows it more than most,' Games said.

'Well it's typical,' Levitch drawled. 'As irresponsible as you're ever goin' to get.'

'I'd say *suicidal*,' Games suggested harshly. 'An' now we'll never know where his share of the loot is, or the identity of his three sidekicks. They're into the next State by now with a few thousand dollars between 'em.'

'We've done all we can,' Levitch muttered. 'There's wires sent to every telegraph office in the territory, but with no descriptions to circulate, they've got it all their own way.'

Games gestured half-heartedly. 'If I hadn't been slowed down with a busted leg . . .' he sighed.

'You think *you'd* have caught him, Myron?'

'I wouldn't have had to,' the sheriff replied snappily. 'I'm frustrated, Dod. It's not every day I discuss losin' a prisoner with a deputy who's already missin' his horse, gun, hat an' coat.'

Levitch pulled the near-empty bottle of physic from his pocket. 'Good job I didn't lose this,' he said. 'Sorry, Myron. The way you put it, it sure sounds crazy.'

'There's no other way to put it. We've just got to get on.' Games glanced out the open window, noted the thin, pink wash of sun up. 'In a couple of days, the boy's pa is comin' to town,' he said. 'You know how familial the Carrick family is. Billy told me he came in for one quick drink, and when he doesn't show, old Harve's goin' to pay us a visit. He'll be expectin' to bail the son who tips Delano's firewater down himself for half the night. Yeah. I'll have to explain why he's now somewhere in the middle of his neighbourhood desert, bitin' dust.'

'Well, I don't have a heap o' pity for the Carrick

clan,' Levitch growled. 'Good-for-nothin' fossickers if you ask me. Everybody knows there's no gold or silver up in those mountain slopes. It's nothin' but goddamn trees, yet they don't wander too far off 'em.'

Unhappily, Games shook his head. 'None of the Carricks have ever been the friendly kind,' he conceded. 'But that ain't against the law. Stubbornness, ain't either. Billy's been the only trouble in the family.'

By early morning, news of Billy Carrick's escape and subsequent disappearance into the Tierra Sin Vida was flowing through Bullhead. Charles Milford stopped by the boarding-house, primarily to check on his patient's progress. Myron Games had no reason for keeping the town doctor ignorant of the whole story and it was soon being passed on.

George Houston heard about it from the waitress in the Land Hotel while working his way leisurely through breakfast. He listened politely but without great interest, had little reason for changing his plans. He was still of a mind to continue his journey northwards, not get concerned with or affected by problems within Bullhead.

It was almost mid-morning when he ambled into the lobby, was greeted by a fretful-looking Orville Land.

'Good morning, Mr Houston, I have a message for you,' the hotel keeper said. 'If you don't mind me saying, after our conversation last night, I'm a tad surprised.'

'And why's that, Mr Land?' Houston inquired, propping a cordial elbow on the reception desk. 'What's happened now?'

'You told me you had no interest in Bullhead's ongoing troubles.'

'That's right. I don't.'

'Then you aren't acquainted with Chester Jarrow's widow?'

'Jarrow, the dead banker? I never heard of him or his wife before.'

Land produced an envelope. 'A boy delivered this while you were eating,' he said.

Houston looked at the letter. 'Hmm, sealed. You're informed on everything but the detail, Mr Land. It's where the devil is . . . apparently.'

'Information can be vital in towns like Bullhead. But it's usually the truth which is written down. I think you're aware of that, Mr Houston.'

Houston took the envelope, noticed the neat handwriting. Mr G. Houston c/o The Land Hotel. He ran a thumb under the flap, extracted the single sheet and read the short letter. 'And it's getting to see those written words that makes it real,' he muttered knowingly. Mindful of Land's curiosity, he reread aloud.

'Dear Mr Houston,
Can you please see your way clear to discuss,

perhaps undertake a personal favour? It concerns a matter which, I am certain, you will be in part, if not fully acquainted with by now. Yours sincerely, Agnes Jarrow.'

Houston folded the note, returned it to its envelope and stowed it in his hip pocket.

'Well, what's to be made of that, I wonder,' Land said.

Houston grinned. 'It's plain enough. Mrs Jarrow wants me to pay her a visit.'

Land gave a slight shake of his head. 'You know what I mean. What's it all about?'

'Accepting you're certain to find out sooner or later, I guess it's going to be about her paying me to find the killer of her husband. If it's anything else, right now and with respect, it's none of your goddamn business. Meantime Mr Land, where do you suggest I go look for her?'

'She's evidently at home,' Land replied, somewhat taken aback at Houston's not ill-humoured response. 'It's the two-storey clapboard at the end of what's called Cottonwood Walk. Turn left out of here, left again at the second corner. It's no more than two or three minutes.'

Houston nodded his thanks and, with a measure of anticipation, adjusted his hat and walked into the morning sunlight.

6

The temperature of the day was already soaring. Houston guessed by noon it would be hot enough to blow the tops off thermometers.

As he passed beneath the half-dozen trees that gave the street its name, he got to thinking of Billy Carrick, pondering the information offered him by the chatty waitress.

A scared youngster would knowingly be headed for a lonely, thirsty death. It was a bad way to go and, although Houston was contemptuous of most murderers, he had a degree of consideration for Billy Carrick.

He lifted the latch of the gate, brushed aside the low branch of a walnut tree, and walked a pebbled path to the portico of the impressive dwelling.

A housemaid answered to his pulling of the door-bell. 'Are you Mr Houston?' she enquired pleasantly.

'Yes, ma'am.' He nodded. 'Maybe a bit sooner than expected.'

'Please come in,' she replied with an accepting smile.

Along a hallway carpeted with Navaho rugs, Houston followed the girl to a small, handsomely-furnished parlour. Seated on a small sofa, a woman gave a word of greeting and made an offer of refreshment. Houston declined, and the woman gestured him to a high-backed chair. He seated himself and, covering a knee with his hat, looked up to meet the intense scrutiny.

Agnes Jarrow was middle-aged with tightly-pinned, ash-grey hair. Her bereavement dress was sombre black that accentuated her pale features. She wore little make-up, and Houston thought her hazel eyes didn't look as though they had suffered from much weeping.

As though reading his thoughts, she lifted her chin to speak. 'You'll know who I am, Mr Houston, no doubt be aware of my circumstances. But I'm no longer weeping. I know nothing will bring my husband back. I shall try to overcome my remaining grief with special memories. He would have wanted it that way, probably be quite proud of me.'

'I'm sure he would, ma'am. Nevertheless, you have my commiserations,' Houston muttered.

'Thank you. I'm glad you didn't say sympathy or pity. And thank you for your prompt response to my note.' Mrs Jarrow settled herself more comfortably.

'Chester has left me well provided for. I can afford to pay well for what I'm going to ask of you. Would you be interested?'

'Not if you were wanting me to harvest your nut trees. But I reckon it's for something more important than that,' he replied, more offhand than he had intended.

'Yes, it's about the jailbreak. April has told me that young Billy Carrick has no food and only one canteen of water. The Tierra Sin Vida has a horrifying reputation and I doubt any local men would follow him in there.'

'Why should they? It would be like chasing him up the scaffold steps. The way I heard it told, there was no doubt about the evidence against him,' Houston said, knowing the answer to his next question before he asked it. 'Likewise, you know something of me, Mrs Jarrow ... my work ... my reputation. So how do I figure here? What would the employment be for?'

'I don't know what kind of man I expected to meet, Mr Houston. I've heard loose talk of similar professional men, but right now, I'm concerned about you holding a confidence,' she murmured.

'If it's about me accepting what it is you're getting around to asking me to do, don't be,' he assured her. 'That's always private.'

Agnes Jarrow smiled contemplatively. 'The people of this town knew Chester Jarrow as a banker, albeit slightly more generous than a typical

one. To me he was a lot more than that, of course
. . . a fine husband with qualities. Never doubt my
loyalty to him, Mr Houston.'

'I have no reason to,' he frowned. 'I trust I'm not
going to.'

'I'm not overcome by thoughts of vengeance, but
I believe his murderers *must* be punished.' She
matched stares with Houston for a long moment,
her voice not faltering as she continued. 'It's the
real murderers I'm talking about, Mr Houston.
They must be caught . . . brought to book for their
brutal, uncivilized crimes.'

Houston nodded thoughtfully. 'Well contrary to
what's put about, there aren't many murderers who
get away with it . . . men *or* women. Like Billy
Carrick who's trapped in a wilderness with little or
no hope of survival. But the three who rode with
him have a chance. They'll probably have split up
. . . riding free and with money for the spending.'

'You believe that?'

'Why not? Their time's limited, though. It'll be
drinking and gambling. The wrong word at the
wrong time in the wrong place. A drunken whisper
in the ear of a pretty saloon girl. Then a lawman
curious about an over-generous stranger. It's the
usual way.'

'You sound as though you know the type well,'
Agnes Jarrow observed.

'I do. Our paths have crossed often enough,'
Houston admitted. 'Sooner or later your husband's

killers will pay the price.'

Agnes Jarrow frowned. 'Hmm. It's the *later*, I don't like. I wouldn't say this to Sheriff Games, nor to Deputy Levitch. Fact is, there's few in Bullhead would actually understand. I'm telling *you*, Mr Houston, because you should be able to be more objective. Being a stranger helps, of course.'

Houston wanted clarification. 'Helps *what*, Mrs Jarrow?' he asked, with a hint of impatience.

'My concern for young Carrick.'

Then, at that moment, Houston realized how she intended her money to be spent. 'I'm not sure I follow you, ma'am,' he said, thinking now he did. 'You'll have to be more specific . . . quite specific.'

Agnes Jarrow's eyes didn't waver, and her voice was level. 'I'm not convinced of Billy Carrick's guilt,' she came out with.

Houston took it in for a moment. 'You can say that, despite the evidence against him?'

'I've given it a lot of thought. The bloody pistol conveniently left beside Chester's body . . . a piece of shirt clutched in his hand. Can you imagine how difficult it actually would have been to obtain that handful-sized piece of shirt, Mr Houston?'

'I hadn't done. But now I think of it, I can see what you mean. Strong evidence though.'

'Too strong. Too contrived and too convenient. That pistol was easily identified as belonging to Billy Carrick. How many murderers would be foolish enough to leave the murder weapon behind? It had his initials on it, for goodness sake.'

'I've listened to some of the talk,' Houston said. 'A drunken murderer's not usually too attentive to detail.'

'Dr Milford gave me a thorough account of the whole, terrible business when I pressed him,' she countered. 'Did you know the boy was found in a back store of Delano's Saloon . . . that he was unconscious when they arrested him? Was *that* in some of the talk, Mr Houston?'

'Not put like that, it wasn't.'

'No. From a virtual lynch mob it wouldn't be, would it? And in this case, the law as well. It's not my area of expertise, but I would have thought that shooting someone might sober you up. Apparently, Billy Carrick did his drinking at the bar, then went into the store room and climbed through a window. There were three strangers waiting outside and he agreed to join them in breaking into the bank.'

Houston was listening silently. He was also breathing deeply, creating images of the incident as Agnes Jarrow continued.

'After shooting my husband dead and arranging the incriminating evidence, he hid his share of cash from the safe and returned to the saloon. Finally, he got comfortable enough to drink himself into near-oblivion and wait for the sheriffs to arrive. Well, Mr Houston, I ask you. If it wasn't for the shocking reality, I'd say it was a turn straight from the music hall.'

For a long moment, Houston thought it over. 'I hadn't even started to consider an alternative state of affairs, ma'am,' he conceded. 'But the way you're telling it now, what's being said does sound too unreasonable to be possible . . . to have happened.'

'You know how a quail walks lamely away from its nest, dragging its wing . . . confusing and attracting attention at the same time? It seems to me that's what we've got here.'

'How'd you mean?'

'The truth was behind the appearance of what happened. There's been a rolling wave of judgement and impulsive action because of it,' she declared. 'As for the Carrick family's animosity towards Chester because he refused them a loan, pah. If that was the custom, there'd be a lot fewer businesses and settlers in Bullhead, I can tell you. But they claim Billy Carrick just hated Chester . . . Chester Jarrow the bank manager, because of it. Well *I* don't believe it.'

'With enough whiskey inside them, any youngster can get to believe almost anything. What's your reason not to?'

Avoiding a categoric answer, Agnes Jarrow continued. 'Naturally I was never a witness to the drinking, those saloon brawls or whatever, but I do have a reason. It's only a one-off, but nevertheless . . .'

'Tell me. If it's personal, it might make a difference to what I do next,' Houston encouraged.

70

For a moment, a slight, meaningful smile melted the sadness of Agnes Jarrow's face. 'It was personal enough,' she started. 'A few months back, there'd been heavy rain all night and all morning, and the main street was a quagmire. I wanted to get across, but the mud was oozing deep. It was Billy Carrick's voice I heard. He was just behind me. Allow me ma'am, he said, and the next thing I knew he was lifting me off the sidewalk and carrying me across the street. Yes, I think he must have had a drink inside him, but it's not the point. It was his instinctive inclination to help, what he said next. Shameless, some would say, but you had to have been there. I *was* and saw something else.'

'Quite the caballero. What *did* he say next?' Houston wanted to know.

'When he set me down on the boardwalk, I thanked him. I'm the wife of Chester Jarrow, the man you're supposed to hate. Did you know that? I asked him.'

' I know who you are, Mrs Jarrow. It don't make the gumbo any less slippy, though, he replied.'

'You didn't think about dropping me in it, then?' I suggested. He shook his head and pushed his hat straight. Naagh. I hate gopher holes an' rain, ma'am . . . 'specially gopher holes filled with rain, he said. But there's no man or woman I can think of. Not livin' anyways. He added that bit in mock toughness. Then he laughed. It left an impression, Mr Houston.'

71

'Yeah, it would.'

'When the murder was discovered, and Billy Carrick was arrested, folk only remembered the bad things, the drinking and street brawling. Some of those people should have known better.'

'I can see how – if it's the same feller we're thinking of – you might feel this way, ma'am,' Houston responded. 'It might all be a falsehood, but that evidence is there and will be considered. . .by the *jury*, not you or me.' Houston looked up at a pair of wall-hung pictures, presumed they were of Mr and Mrs Jarrow. 'Of course, there have been cases where evidence was proved to have been planted,' he said.

'I suppose,' she murmured disconsolately.

'Now perhaps you can tell me what it is you want me to do,' he said, attempting to bring up the mood dip.

'If that boy is guilty, it must be decided in a court of law, not by some crude, arcane justice,' Agnes Jarrow said. 'He must be given every opportunity to plead his case . . . to be defended by a proficient attorney. If he *is* innocent, as opposed to not being proved guilty, he shouldn't be left to die in that dreadful wasteland.'

It was close to what Houston was thinking. 'Fair enough. And you're asking me to go after him? You want him brought back alive to stand trial?'

'Yes, Mr Houston. For that I'm prepared to pay you one thousand dollars. The Tierra Sin Vida deserves its bleak reputation, but I believe if you're properly prepared and there's an attractive enough reward, you'll have the beating of it. There'll be maps at the Land Office, not that there'll be any helpful information on them, and I'll pay for a pack animal . . . two if you need them.'

Houston grinned wryly. 'You done much man hunting before, ma'am?'

'It seems to me, you find out why men die, then do your best to counter it,' she responded. 'It would be an outrage for Chester's murderers to evade punishment. Worse if an innocent man went to his death because of it. In that, my motive is clear. And I'm not overlooking the fact that the law is implicated,' she added sharply.

Houston picked up his hat, got to his feet and walked to the door. 'In some ways, young Carrick's got a lot going for him. Someone like you, grubstaking his life with most of it ahead of him.'

'It's not a grubstake, Mr Houston. Does that mean you'll go after him?'

'Just as soon as I get myself that proper preparation. And for a thousand dollars, I'll do most things straightaway.'

'Thank you. He's carrying the deputy sheriff's sidearm, apparently.' Agnes Jarrow stifled the weakest of grins. 'So he may resist.'

'They sometimes do, given a chance. Don't worry, ma'am, it comes with the territory. I'll bring him back alive.'

7

Orville Land directed Houston to a stock dealer, advised him of the store for supplies. The hotel-keeper also attempted to deter him from the venture.

'It'll be like suicide,' he warned.

'Just how big is it then, this desert?' Houston asked. 'More than a thousand miles across?'

'Not quite. But it'll probably seem like it. I once read, it's the cautious who make fewer mistakes.'

'Well I wouldn't want being cautious to be my downfall. I've got all the essential trappings to survive.'

'You'll have more than food and drink to worry about,' Land persisted. 'What happens if you meet up with Carrick sooner than you thought. Don't forget he's got some knowledge of the place, could be laying for you ... for *someone* right now. He's already half lizard if you ask me. Do you really want to die out there on the sandy griller, watching your blood burn as it leaks away? It's a mighty curious move for someone looking for a cooler destination.'

'I'll admit it don't sound too welcoming. But sometimes in my business, Mr Land, you get paid a sum of money that's worth dying for. Maybe we can discuss the imprudence of that on my return.'

'Sure. *Me and my business* will still be up and running,' Orville sighed.

A clerk at the Land Office supplied Houston with a map section of the territory. The document indicated Tierra Sin Vida, and hill country to the north. Houston gave a spare smile at another inclusion . . . the Bullhead graveyard. He then visited the corral to discuss the hiring of a suitable pack mule, and his provender was purchased at Furr's Mercantile. Houston wasn't too exacting, told the merchant he could live off coffee and walnuts if he had to. When Houston rode from Bullhead, half a dozen canteens and a couple of skin bags were slung over the mule's back. He set a medium pace with his grullo mare, the pack mule tagging close.

Within fifteen minutes of Houston leaving town, Deputy Levitch was finding out what he needed to know. A casual enquiry from Abraham Furr was gaining him vital information.

'Sure, he was here,' the storekeeper told him. 'Took enough supplies for a whole convention o' goddamn bounty hunters. Didn't say where, but I'll bet every dollar comes through here today, he's ridin' after Billy Carrick. Why'd he want so many canteens an' them skin-bags? Hell, he's totin' enough water to set up home in that godforsaken place. Then again, maybe it's just for half-way an' back. What d'you reckon, Dod?'

'I reckon he's a sharp son-of-a-bitch,' Levitch said, for Furr's benefit. 'Bullhead law needs no help from the likes o' him. He was warned not to butt in.'

Dod Levitch considered riding out to talk with Fats Denvy or Jack Carboys, then, figuring it an assignment he should handle alone, decided against. Soon, he was leaving town on his own, not on Houston's trail, but headed north-west and shielded by sagebrush that ringed half the town.

By mid-afternoon he had reached his vantage point. It was a flat-topped mesa, from where he commanded a sweeping view of the area to the south and west of the headwater creek. He had pushed his mount hard, and estimated he had made it with time to spare. It would be a long-range shot, but in the still air, Levitch had faith in the accuracy of his aim, the carrying power of the .44 Winchester.

Reaching the east bank, Houston reined in, dismounted to look more closely at the run of the creek. He was a mile upstream of where Levitch had found evidence of Carrick taking on water. The creek was narrower, running faster and occasionally deeper, and carried the general detritus of distant timberlands. It was all turning and drifting south in its flow towards Lake Mead and the mighty Colorado. Nevertheless, Houston thought the water looked clean enough for drinking.

He got to work filling the two canteens. He lashed the six extras and the two skin bags to his saddle, took comfort from the small sacks of coffee and corn dodgers tied to the mule's back.

As he remounted he stared across to the far bank, beyond to where the infamous, desolate expanse of wasteland began. He nudged the mare on, seeking shallower water to make a crossing together with the pack mule.

In the lonely almost spooky stillness, and for some inexplicable reason, the warning words of Orville Land suddenly entered Houston's consciousness. He looked for sign of Carrick, for anybody, even movement from Gila monsters or deadly, water snakes.

He was half-way across, peering into the shadows of boulder shelves on the opposite bank when, with the simultaneous crack of a rifle, he felt the heavy pulse of a bullet thumping past his neck. Almost as though he knew it was coming, he threw up a hand, pitched sideways from his saddle, down to the roil of water.

He took a gulping breath, then there was a

deeper silence as the numbing shock of water closed above him, the stunning contrast to the high heat of the afternoon. He saw the dark, waving reach of a large branch above him, for a few seconds kicked out, then clawed with his arms. He surfaced slowly, his head pressing up through fronds still thick with young pine cones. He drifted, gasping for breath, but apparently unscathed, hoping the foliage was shielding him from the sight of his would-be assassin.

Levitch laid the rifle aside. Reaching for his spyglass he studied the stretch of water to the south. He was satisfied that, with one carefully aimed shot, his victim had fallen like he'd seen in his mind's eye. For a full minute he peered down from the butte, but there was little movement, save the swirl of timbered snags. 'He died. Even if I winged him, he's drowned dead. Leave 'em no evidence, Doddy,' he muttered to himself.

Five minutes later, still drifting but treading water, Houston raised his head above the needled fronds and looked around him. The mare and the mule had crossed the creek, were standing on the west bank with their heads hanging forlornly.

As his ears cleared and hearing returned, he listened intently, was certain he heard the far-off, indistinct clip of a horse's hoof. *You've tried your best,* he thought. *Riding away's your big mistake.* For a moment, he wondered if it could have been Carrick's erstwhile friends, whether all, or just one of them had turned back ... if he was now up against three or four guns.

'If it's a handful of you, fine. If you're a lone shooter, hard goddamn luck,' he muttered aloud. 'I'll find you, but you don't know it. That's my edge, you son-of-a-bitch.' Meantime, Billy Carrick was a fugitive on the Tierra Sin Vida, and his time was running out, he reminded himself. Pushing away the pine debris he reached for the bank, moments later stepping from the shallows onto dry land.

He dragged his hat from his belt where he'd shoved it after hitting the water. He pushed and pulled it about until it resembled its shape; satisfied, adjusted it on his head.

By the time Houston reached his mare, his clothes were giving off a light mist. *Some folk pay good money to John Woo's bath house for this treatment,* he couldn't help thinking. A hot wind gusted towards him from the desert and the grullo nickered a greeting. He patted high on its shoulder and smiled relief, made a few reassuring sounds.

With his mind now sharpened, he swung into the saddle, squinting against the glare of the bleached sand, keeping the pace easy to conserve the stamina of his animals. The surprise ambush was a needed reminder. It warned of a quarry's ability as well as their whereabouts. He wondered again who it might be, didn't have enough background to make

79

a list or reasoned assessment.

The low, curling currents of air lacked the strength to wipe out tracks left by the stolen horse, and for Houston, a few hours trailing was clear-cut.

That night he didn't think twice about making a small, camp fire. Fifty feet from where he lit his kindling, a pillar of basalt rock rose high to overlook miles in every direction. The best vantage-point around here, he decided. There's rattlers at the foot and I'm watching out for all of you. 'So if you think you'll be safe up there ... go ahead feller, whoever you are,' he warned quietly, then continued to wipe dry and clean his Colt.

The desert crossing promised to be a tiring business. But his attitude was improved, furthered by dragging a soogan around him and drinking hot coffee spiked from a small flask of Jamaica rum.

In the early morning, despite the already rising heat, Houston felt refreshed and equal to who and whatever lay ahead of him.

He resumed his pursuit, again without urgency but with heightened vigilance. His mare was faring well and the rimrock mule gave no trouble. At midday, under the shade of slanting bedrock, he ate four corn dodgers and drank tepid water. It was a ten-minute break, instead of a nooning with hot coffee. He felt sure Carrick would be slowed down by pushing a horse into a too-anxious run across the savage, debilitating terrain. Although he recalled Orville Land telling him the boy would be at home in any devil's kitchen, it didn't stretch to Levitch's bay mare. By maintaining a steady pace, Houston calculated he could reach the fugitive while still alive.

At three o' clock he found the horse at the foot of a long, rock-strewn bench. It was still saddled, and Houston's arrival sent the turkey vultures soaring skyward. He wanted to use his rifle, but knew he couldn't. The mare's left foreleg was obviously broken, probably in a tumble from weariness while descending the bench. It was too late for the animal. Carrick had put it out of its misery, and Houston now felt a twinge of consideration for him.

He wasn't following the tracks of a horse any longer, just the heel and toe boot impressions from a weak, stumbling man. At the approach of first dark, Houston felt a tinge of frustration that he hadn't yet caught sight of him. It wasn't until full dark had shrouded the desert that he reined.

He made cold-harbour camp and slept soundly, rising and stretching at sun-up for a simple breakfast. He continued to trail west, and the next time he checked his pocket-watch, it was mid-morning and there was movement ahead of him on the western horizon. Just left of the brilliant orb of the rising sun, he could see the big, lazily-circling birds were staying high. It probably meant Carrick was still on his feet, maybe even on the move. If the vultures swooped, he would heel the mare from an

81

easy trot to something faster.

One hour later he reined in the mare, listened to the sounds that seemed to emanate from the bed of a dried-up scrape ahead of him.

'That's as far as you come, mister . . . if you're yearnin' to stay alive.' The warning voice was weak with exhaustion, just about audible.

Houston rose in the stirrups and squinted ahead to where his quarry waited. There was little cover, and Houston was guessing he'd probably collapsed, and being too weak to go on, decided to attempt a last stand.

'Stay put, kid, and don't do anything stupid,' Houston called out. 'If you feel anything like me, you're almost finished,' he lied. 'I'm walking in now, so if you're holding any kind of gun . . . any weapon, those vultures are having you as fine fixings. Besides, I got enough fresh water to re-float the Merrimack,' he added, riding forward another thirty yards.

When he swung down from the mare, he took handcuffs and a pigging string from his saddle pouch of trade requisites. He drew his Colt, walked slowly, cautiously to the crusty lip of the scrape.

Against a boulder in the centre of the hollow, Billy Carrick was on his knees, trying for his feet. Dod Levitch's Colt and a stub knife lay in front of him. He was gasping, and his once-tanned face was streaked white from the alkali sticking to his sweat.

'You were saying, kid?' Houston started dryly.

'You just stay as you are. I'll give you something soon as you're wearing these cuffs.'

'Then what'll you do to me?' Carrick gasped wearily.

Houston didn't answer. He snapped the handcuffs around the man's wrists, knotted one end of the rawhide to the steel centre link and stepped back.

Carrick's legs buckled as he tried to get to his feet. 'I can't stand. I already killed a goddamn horse for the same thing,' he mumbled miserably.

Houston went to fetch his mare and the pack mule, used his soogan to fend off the high sun. Carrick lay beneath it, trembling, muttering incoherently until Houston let him have one of the canteens. 'When you're full, go to sleep,' he advised. 'It won't seem quite as bad.'

'Will I wake up from the sound o' you shootin' me? Who the hell are you anyway?' Carrick asked, his voice almost disappearing.

'I'll tell you when food's ready.' Houston started a fire, contemplated a meal of pozole and beans and strong, scalding coffee.

A few hours later, Houston handed Carrick another canteen of water, then poured a mug of coffee fortified by a slug of his rum.

'Now you can tell me who you are,' Carrick said, once his hunger and thirst were sated. 'You don't seem to be carryin' any sort o' badge.'

'My name's George Houston. Some call me a regulator, others a law adjuster. I guess most would call me a bounty hunter.' Houston then gave a brief explanation of his arrival, subsequent activity in Bullhead. 'So, I'm here because Chester Jarrow's widow thinks maybe you're not so guilty. She offered me a real big reward to bring you back.'

'Jarrow's widow? Yeah, I seem to recall her. She didn't seem the kind o' lady who'd post bounty on anyone.' Carrick shrugged. 'Huh, I guess she's like all the others though,' he said dejectedly.

'It's possible. But the others ain't paying big money to find out,' Houston replied sharply. He took out his map and unfolded it. 'According to this, we're past half way. I figure we can make our rations and water last, but only by heading towards Lake Mead.'

'That'll be the Black Mountains. I know 'em,' Carrick sighed. 'Timberland an' lots o' good water. Seems a long ways off right now.'

'There's a trail leads from the foothills to Bullhead,' Houston observed.

'Yeah, the haulage road. I know it,' Carrick muttered. 'Travelled it every time I rode to an' from town.'

'But not this time,' Houston suggested.

'Goddamn right. Figured no man would have the grit to follow me in here. Territory folk reckon it's possessed. But you're a stranger . . . wouldn't make any difference. 'Course you were goin' to catch up with me.'

84

Houston pushed Dod Levitch's Colt back in its holster, coiled the belt and stowed it in a saddle pouch. 'I'll shift some of the load off the mule,' he told Carrick. 'That's for you. It's extra weight for both, but now you're improved we can walk some.'

'We?' Carrick repeated. 'You forgettin' I'm Billy Carrick the killer who beat ol' Jarrow to death with his gun? That I helped three desperados rob the town of its money, then spent my share on Delano's goddamn cocktails? What chance have I got back there?'

'I've never brought anyone back dead,' Houston retorted. 'Not unless they wanted it that way. Then I'd oblige.'

'You'd be obligin' *me*. Hell, you must've seen 'em in the streets . . . like a pack o' wild dogs treein' a coon. Why not put a bullet in me right now and be done with it? Cut me like I did the bay, why don't you?'

'Because I'm being paid to take you back alive. Now rest your mouth while I get these animals ready to move us out.'

Houston rearranged the remaining loads until there was room for Carrick to sit astride the mule. He helped Carrick to mount; taking one end of the reins, he secured it to the grullo's saddle-horn and swung into the saddle.

'Knowing this territory the way you do, maybe you can say how long it'll take us to get out of it,' he said as they walked the animals from the shallow scrape.

Carrick made a simple calculation. 'If we make camp when the sun goes down . . . start off again when it comes up, we could be into the hills by noon,' he muttered. 'We could make it sooner, but not if we're sparin' these mounts.'

'If we ride them non-stop we might never get any place,' Houston rasped. 'Are there homesteaders in those hills?' he wanted to know.

'Yeah, some. Why?'

'If I can make a deal for a couple of saddle-brokes, we can ride to Bullhead easier,' Houston said.

'Reckon I know a place,' Carrick replied, but not clear enough for Houston to hear.

From then on, Carrick had little to say. He was generally uncommunicative, clearly of troubled mind. 'You ain't the law, not judge nor jury either,' he pointed out. 'You're just someone who hunts men for the price on their heads. What do you care if they're innocent or guilty? You get paid either way.'

'Well, Mrs Jarrow thinks you might be innocent,' Houston pointed out. 'Unless you got some other story, why not try and convince me?'

'Waste o' breath. Sides, I'm too tired,' Carrick replied. He remained morose and preoccupied through their supper and into the start of the night.

With Carrick so fatigued, as well as being expertly

tied, Houston managed to get some sleep, albeit fitful. At dawn he revived their fire and prepared a substantial breakfast.

'Eat it. You'll get so lean the noose'll slip straight to your boots.'

Carrick cursed Houston, but ate. It was more mechanical than appreciative, as though he was getting resigned to the inevitable, sick with a sense of the waiting gallows.

8

That morning the temperature rose high. Their clothes hugged tight and clammy. Their thirst was huge, but Houston was managing the situation. They drank in moderation, attentively watched the skin bags. Houston wasn't unduly concerned. He knew that even if the water ran out, they could make it for a further day and night before real trouble set in.

The last of the canteens was still half-full when they emerged from the parched plateau. A few hundred yards ahead Houston could see the green, leafy swathes of juniper and aspen of the Black Mountain foothills.

'Looks like we made it,' he commented calmly. 'I guess it could've been a lot worse.'

'How'd you figure that?' Carrick said. 'Right now, worse is me gettin' my neck stretched.'

'I meant you got the timing right for here,'

Houston acknowledged. 'Without looking at my watch, I'd say it was just about noon.'

'So, what happens now?' Carrick asked.

'Like I said . . . find the nearest saddlers to hire . . . buy if I have to. My mare's got real bad feet.'

Further into the hills, Houston called a halt to examine the hoofs of the mounts. He cleared gravel from the hoof pads of the grullo, but knew it was only temporary relief.

'Get down,' he told Carrick. 'We'll lead them from here on.' He took the mare's reins and the mule's tie rope, and indicated that Carrick walk ahead of him.

When they came across the narrow path of a hunter, they stayed with it for about a mile. Then, still some distance ahead, Houston saw the slender, climbing ribbon of white smoke. He was about to point it out when Carrick spoke.

'I saw it before you did,' he said.

'It's not from a campfire.'

'Nope,' Carrick agreed. 'It's a regular smoke-stack.'

'Means someone's at home. Keep headed towards it,' Houston said.

Carrick trudged on with his head bowed, his hands clasped and cuffed behind him. Houston was gripping the mare's reins and tie rope in his left hand, his Colt now in his right.

Soon the cabin appeared dead ahead. It was a rudimentary logged structure with a thick, sod roof, but somewhat larger, more robust than usual. There was a pole corral containing several horses.

In the shadow of the rising hill, the encampment area had a permanent appearance. Thirty yards up the hillside, Houston saw the unmistakeable prop structure of a mine shaft.

A man was already climbing from the corral, hustling towards them with an irate challenge. He was toting a scatter-gun and Houston judged him to be middle-aged. He was garbed in home-spuns, sweat-grimed range hat and boots. Another, and much older man was emerging from the mine shaft. His hair was silver-grey, but in all other respects similar appearance to the first man and he held a big, Patterson Colt. Houston, with no reason to expect a hostile reception, other than a miner's customary aversion to unannounced strangers, quickly forgot his weariness.

'Hold it fellers. A gunfight seems a hell of a price to pay for making a mistake,' he called.

'Billy boy,' shouted back the man with the scatter-gun. 'What in tarnation's all this?'

'Swing around him, Gramps,' Carrick yelled to the older man. 'I don't reckon he'll shoot.'

'Don't bet anyone's life on it, boy,' Houston rasped. 'He knows he'll be the first to die.'

The scatter-gun man stopped, for a moment uncertain. 'Who's this, Billy?' he questioned. 'Where the hell you been? Step forward. Let's see you.'

Before anything happened, Houston's uncertainty increased when two women came out of the cabin. One was tall and of similar age to the man with the scatter-gun. The moment she saw Billy Carrick, the mien of her face showed shock and dismay. The other woman appeared to be hardly out of her teens. She was short, slightly built and very fair-haired. Her tiny, right fist gripped what Houston thought might have been a match to the Patterson Colt.

'Whoever you are, you best drop that nice-lookin' Colt. We got the majority here,' called out the man with the scatter gun. 'It won't be much of a gunfight.'

'Just watch him careful, Pa,' Billy Carrick warned. 'He's smart . . . quick as a coachwhip.'

'Pa?' Houston repeated incredulously, then flicked a glance towards the older man outside the shaft entrance. 'Gramps? Hell, you mean *your* grandpa? And this is your pa?'

'Yeah. Your smartness must have taken a couple o' minutes off, Houston,' Billy Carrick sneered. 'You've brought me home. Say howdy to my folks.'

'So, drop your piece, mister,' called the fair-haired girl. 'Drop it an' move away from my brother or . . . or . . .'

'Or nothin', Mimsy,' Billy's father interrupted. 'Now hush up.'

'Reckon I have indeed made a mistake, Mr Carrick, assuming that's your name,' Houston said.

91

'But please don't get in the way of my intention. I'm only interested in horses.'

'The boy's handcuffed,' Gramps observed. 'But the stranger ain't puttin' up a tin star. Maybe he's one o' them out o' State kidnappers.'

'He's George Houston, not a goddamn thief,' Billy explained and grinned derisively. 'He's a bounty hunter.'

'So how come you's his prisoner?' his father demanded.

'I can explain that,' Houston replied. 'But only after you lower those shooters. That goes for you too, ma'am.'

'We got him outnumbered an' surrounded,' the old timer reminded his family. 'How come he's callin' the shots?'

'He's got the drop on Billy an' can't miss from where he's standin'. That's why,' Billy's father answered back.

'Your son's wanted for murder, and I'm aiming to take him back to Bullhead for trial,' Houston announced. He felt uncomfortable and apprehensive, sorry for the woman who silently clasped her hands to her mouth. Carrick's sister, Mimsy, gasped and let the old revolver drop from her fingers. In turn, his father and grandfather lowered their weapons.

'I don't want any trouble from you people,' Houston went on. 'If I'd known I was headed for Billy's home, I'd have changed direction, and that's the truth of it.'

The Carrick family eyed him in bemused silence. The girl was first to speak.

'Is it, Billy? Is it true what he says?' she asked, staring worriedly at her brother.

'Yeah. I'm wanted for murder all right. But I didn't do it, Sis, an' nobody's goin' to believe me.'

Mimsy gripped her mother's arm and walked her past the corral. Gramps Carrick descended the slope to stand beside his son.

Houston holstered his Colt and told Billy he could rest up a while. 'I reckon now's your time,' he said. 'They're entitled to some sort of explanation. Tell them.'

Billy sat on a juniper blowdown. In brief, affecting sentences he acquainted his family with his predicament. They listened, attentive to every word, every nuance and expression. When he'd finished, he grinned wryly at Houston, then his family. 'So, this is George Houston. He can't help what he is. Bit like us.'

'I'm sorry we have to get introduced like this,' Houston told them.

'He talks like someone schooled,' Mimsy observed.

'I'm just naturally careful ... guarded mostly,' Houston replied.

'Feller does what you do, I ain't surprised,' Gramps contributed dourly.

Houston nodded. 'There's no other way,' he said.

'If your boy's innocent he'll be back the sooner for it.'

'I *am* innocent, goddamnit. Sorry, Sis . . . Ma,' Billy growled. 'But how can I prove it?'

'Nevada,' Gramps stated. 'Once he's across the line, Utah law can't touch him.'

'I could,' Houston responded. 'I gave up respecting County and State borders many years ago. It's something you don't want to test me on.'

'No, I bet. Runnin' anywhere ain't goin' to help him any,' Harve Carrick said. 'Besides, I don't want my son to be called a killer on the loose.' For a moment he stared hard at Houston. 'Have every lawman an' goddamn bounty hunter west o' the Grand Canyon wantin' to collar him. No, the boy has to be cleared, else none of us will be able to show our faces in Bullhead again.'

'All my family deaf?' Billy challenged. 'They've got evidence. They found my gun by Jarrow's body. He had a piece o' my shirt in his fist. Hell, I'm still wearin' it.'

'You say you were so drunk you can't recall anythin' that happened?' Harve put to Billy. 'Huh, it's the bit I'd believe.'

'Yeah, an' it's the truth. I know it ain't a defence, but it's what happened.'

'What we goin' to do, Harve?' Billy's mother asked distraughtly.

'Not sure, Alice. Us Carricks are supposed to be wild an' unfriendly . . . spend most nights at the jar, some say. But that ain't so,' Harve muttered. 'We ain't makin' a fortune from this claim . . . hell we ain't makin' a pinch. But we're workin' at it . . . hopin' for a bonanza one day.'

'That's an OK sentiment, Mr Carrick, but what's it mean? Why are you telling *me*?' Houston asked.

'I'm tellin' you so's you know. For all the tarra-diddle about us, we never went against the law. Maybe Myron Games don't trust us, but that ain't our fault. We're as law abidin' as any pasty-faced towners . . . maybe more so.'

'Got no reason not to believe you,' Houston accepted.

'An' the boy *still* won't have a chance.' Gramps scowled.

'But we've got to see if there's one there, Gramps,' Harve answered. 'I don't cotton to that sheriff, but repute says he's a square-shooter.'

'If that's how you feel, you can oblige me,' Houston said. 'I need a couple of saddle-brokes.'

Harve nodded. 'I've got 'em.'

'And give me your word you won't help the boy escape. You know that if you do, any understandings are off, and that's not good for your Billy or you. We'll stay here until morning, and in return I'll give you an assurance.'

'On what?'

'I'll take the boy back alive. But just to get it all clear, what I'm doing is my business, how I earn money, so by Christ, I *am* taking him. There'll be no

95

mob lynching and I'll even check on a local lawyer, if there is such a thing.' Houston switched his attention to the mother and daughter, offered a slight reassuring grin. 'No matter what you've heard of people like me, my bounty's paid on bringing back young Billy alive.'

'I believe him, Pa,' Mimsy said.

'Got no choice,' Harve conceded. 'I figure he'll do right by us, but he's only one man. Those who want to hang young Billy, come by the handful. You can stay with us tonight, Mr Houston. An' tomorrow when you move out, some of us will be right alongside you.'

Harve swung up his scatter-gun but Houston shook his head emphatically. 'No, Mr Carrick, you've been misunderstanding me. I'm not taking anyone else along. It's just me and Billy.'

9

Harve Carrick gave Houston a long, severe look. 'An' how'd you reckon on stoppin' us?' he demanded. 'The east trail's for anyone to use. I ain't your prisoner, nor's Gramps or the women. So how can you stop us from just taggin' along?'

'Who's goin' to cook for you?' Ma asked.

'An' tuck you in at night?' Mimsy added.

'You all just haul in,' Houston rejoined. 'I'm taking in a fugitive of the law, not his whole family.'

Gramps Carrick fidgeted with irritation. 'Like Harve says, how can you stop us?' he asked, adding something unintelligible.

'Ne'er mind him. He's just lookin' for trouble,' Harve said. 'Your word an' mine should be good enough. We won't give you no trouble, Mr Houston. We just have to be sure there's some look out for young Billy.'

'Yeah. Pity you didn't think like that before he

took to the bottle, Mr Carrick,' Houston answered back.

Harve Carrick warped a smile. 'I guess I deserve that,' he said. 'Perhaps I'm tryin' to make up.'

Houston shrugged. 'As good a time as any.'

'I'll make us all some food then. Come with me, Mimsy,' Ma announced. She retreated to the cabin with her daughter while Harve and the old man helped Houston unpack the grullo mare and the pack mule. Houston realized the Carrick clan were accepting the inevitable, Gramps even becoming gruffly polite. Harve gave him a nubbin of lye soap and a towel, nodded towards a barrel at a corner of the corral. After some hesitation, he unlocked Billy's handcuffs, gave a look that represented don't try anything I won't like.

Houston was vaguely disturbed when they asked him to sit at one end of their table. He suspected it was so they could all keep an eye on him, for some reason.

Ma sensed his unease. 'When you're on the trail you'll be the man takin' away our Billy,' she said. 'When you're here eatin' with us, you're a guest.'

Houston considered the words, thought there was a challenge. In some way he felt less comfortable, even more so when Harve said a rudimentary grace.

Mimsy and her mother served up tasty platters of meat, gravy and sourdough biscuits. There was an unreal atmosphere to this brief period of domesticity. Their attitude was summed up by Harve.

'We got no right to treat Mr Houston bad,' he said. 'If he was, he wouldn't be returnin' Billy the way he says he is. Even though we'll be watchin'.'

As if reading all their thoughts, Mimsy chimed in. 'They only hang guilty men. Ain't that so, Mr Houston?'

'Generally speaking, yes. It's the usual arrangement.' Houston was at once thinking that there had always been exceptions to the rule.

'Well then, all will be fine,' the girl smiled, then immediately changed the subject. 'I'll bet you've travelled all over, Mr Houston. Have you seen the really big towns, like Cedar City an' Colorado Springs? I'm goin' to travel when I'm older. I want to visit one of those fancy theatres with terpsichore an' dancin' an' play-actin' on a stage with coloured lamps an' all. When I get to be twenty-one, Pa's sendin' me to stay with my Aunt Clara in Kansas City. She sends me newspapers an' pictorials an' . . .'

'Stop gabblin' on, Mimsy,' Ma intervened. 'Mr Houston's got other stuff to think about. Let him finish his food.'

Meanwhile, the sharp-eyed Gramps had been looking at Houston's hat. It was hanging on one of the big clout nails near the parlour entrance, beside the Stetson Billy had taken from Dod Levitch.

'That bonnet o' yours has sure taken a bashin',' he pointed out. 'Why's it lookin' more like a drowned cat?'

Houston smiled ruefully as the memory returned. It hadn't occurred to him to tell Billy about the sharpshooter at the creek. 'Somebody took a shot at me before I started into the desert. I spent some time under the water . . . me and my hat.'

Billy grinned. 'Hah, I guess nobody cares much for a bounty hunter.'

'So you didn't see who it was?' Harve wondered.

'Hardly.' Houston grinned crookedly. 'But he likely figures I'm floating face down towards Mexico.'

'An old enemy maybe?' Harve pressed.

Houston shrugged. 'Don't narrow it down much. Could be one of a few.'

'If I was you, feller, I'd be a mighty jumpy hombre,' Gramps grunted.

'It's something for me to think about. But it can wait until I've taken your Billy back to Bullhead.'

'Yeah, nothin's more important than one hundred sawbucks,' Billy joined in.

'Who was it made such a big offer?' Harve asked.

'Agnes Jarrow . . . Chester Jarrow's wife. She got to thinking Billy is innocent,' Houston told him.

'But why. . . ?' Ma started.

'Because she knew he'd die unless somebody went after him with water and supplies.' Houston frowned at Harve. 'Mrs Jarrow feels like you do, Mr Carrick. She's expecting Billy to be cleared when he stands trial.'

100

'*If* he stands trial, more like,' Billy scowled.

'It was a real Christian thing she did,' Ma reflected. 'Forgettin' her own grief to do it.'

'I don't think she's forgot *that*, Mrs Carrick.' Houston wondered if, for the shortest moment, he was considering Agnes Jarrow's common sense rather than the palpable evidence.

Conversation broke up until the end of the meal. When they were chewing their way through thick coffee, Harve opened up on his thinking.

'Look, Mr Houston, you an' my boy ain't *that* tired,' he said. 'So why wait till tomorrow mornin'? We all want Billy squared with the law, an' as soon as can be done. So why don't we pull out straight away?'

'My thinkin' too,' Gramps readily agreed.

'We could all be ready in less than an hour,' Mort continued. 'There's no rich pickin's to guard. What we got's transferable assets . . . can be carried in our pockets. You'll be back in town sooner'n it took to cross the Tierra Sin Vida.'

Houston's brows knitted with unease. He wondered if he was being finagled . . . having his ropes pulled.

Billy grinned mirthlessly. 'Why not? Why wait, Houston?' he asked. 'You'll be itchin' to get your hands on all that bounty.'

'Just stop it, Billy,' his mother sighed. 'Things are the way they are. Let's get on with what's to be done.'

101

Houston stared hard at his captive. 'I'll leave the cuffs off,' he told him coldly. 'You're a born tear-away. But you're not doing it between here and Bullhead. And before a smirk creases your face, it's more for your ma than what *you* might be thinking.'

'Don't worry,' Harve growled. 'If he runs, I'll catch him . . . take my belt to him, if I have to.'

'Whose side you on, Pa?' Billy challenged.

'Your ma's . . . like Mr Houston. Maybe someday you'll understand why we're wantin' to get you cleared.'

'There ain't an attorney in this whole blessed country who could talk a jury into turnin' *me* loose,' Billy muttered. 'How'd he explain my gun bein' in the bank with Jarrow's blood all over it? An' my shirt . . .'

Houston cut him short. 'Save it. We'll have time enough for coming up with something.'

'Ma an' Gramps an' Mimsy can ride in the wagon. The team's sound . . . can move smart if we have to,' Harve said. 'I've got horses for you, me an' Billy. I don't know of anyone round these parts snaky enough to steal your mare or the mule.'

Houston nodded. 'So, we'll start as soon as you folks are ready.'

They were moving away from the Carrick place within an hour. The charcoal mare loaned to Houston, lacked the grullo's breeding, but it was well broken and easy to manage. Houston was riding alongside Billy, some fifty feet behind Harve. After them came the freighter drawn by the pair of teamsters. Gramps was handling the reins and Mimsy and Ma perched beside him on the seat. It doubled as a locker, most likely contained the Carrick arsenal of fully functional weapons.

'Reckon we'll meet the Bullhead trail in another hour,' Harve called over his shoulder.

Houston nodded, took another preoccupied look at Billy. 'I meant to mention it before,' he started. 'That's quite a hat. A tad out of place on you.'

'That's 'cause it's Levitch's.' Billy grinned. 'You hear how I'd cleared jail?'

'Sure, I heard. Dressed in the deputy's best duds. I just mentioned it.'

'I guess he'll be real pleased to get it back. An' maybe he's picked up his fancy buckskin jacket. I knew I wouldn't need it where I was headed.'

'From what I heard, you could just as easily have got away by the rear door of that jail,' Houston suggested. 'You had Levitch's keys. What's more, the main street wasn't too quiet. It was packed with marauding neck-tie party goers. I'd hate to think what would have happened if you'd been spotted.'

'But I wasn't,' Billy returned. 'They saw the pretty hat an' jacket an' made a deputy sheriff out of it.'

'So why take the risk?'

Billy rubbed his chin, did some thinking. 'Not real sure . . . difficult to remember right back. But

103

there was somethin' . . . somethin' wrong.'

'No surprise you can't remember. Word was, you were more drunk than a skunk.'

'What do *they* all know? *I know* I only had two shots at Delano's,' Billy claimed. 'It's all I had payment for, an' they don't exactly keep a runnin' tab. How the hell did I get to feel so bad? There's somethin' wrong there, too. I'll keep thinkin' though . . . it'll come to me.'

By mid-afternoon they reached the town trail, pushed on eastward at a slightly faster pace. Under different circumstances, Houston might have travelled on through the night, but they still managed to cover ten miles before first dark. Harve advised them to make camp under the foliage cover of an aspen break, forty or fifty yards off the trail. After the horses had been fed and watered, rubbed down and staked out, Gramps helped Mimsy and her ma get a fire going, make ready for the evening meal.

There was little in the way of conversation after supper, just personal doubts and uncertainties. To the consternation of her pa, Mimsy seemed eager to draw Houston into talking about his adventurous career.

'You an' your ma sleep in the wagon,' Harve told her. 'Mr Houston, do we post a guard?'

Gramps didn't wait to hear Houston's reply. 'Goddamn right we do,' he gruffed. 'How do we know we ain't goin' to run into one o' them Bullhead posses? They were too blame scared to chase Billy across the wilderness, an' it's likely some of 'em guessed he'd head for home.'

'Some people seemed sure Billy would never make that crossing,' Houston recalled.

'An' some probably heard him braggin' that he ain't scared on account o' there bein' a couple o' sink holes. They might remember that,' Harve said.

'So, they'd ride this here trail,' Gramps insisted. 'They'd be figurin' to wait for him on the other side.'

'It makes *some* sort of sense,' Houston agreed. 'But *no* sense in taking chances. I'll take the first lookout until midnight. Reckon I can hold out that long.'

'Yeah. Wake me up then,' Harve offered. 'I'll be under the wagon.' He eyed his son unhappily. 'I guess you'll want Billy close enough for you to see him . . . close to the fire?'

Houston confirmed with a nod. 'That would be best,' he said.

10

Harve and Gramps were rolled in blankets beneath the freighter. The two women remained inside, and Billy was hunkered by the fire, staring sullenly into the flames. Houston slid his Winchester from its sheath, and settled down opposite him. The wagon was out of earshot, but they spoke quietly.

'Sort o' weird . . . grisly, but every mile we travel takes me closer to bein' human fruit,' Billy reflected.

'You aren't the most hopeful man I ever took in, young feller,' Houston replied. 'There's more than one way of looking ahead.'

'How many ways is a judge an' jury goin' to look? Hell, there's nobody left in Bullhead don't want me hung.'

'There you go again. Have you remembered, yet?'

'About what?'

'You said it would come to you . . . why you didn't

go out the back door of the jailhouse. Why you chose the front?'

Billy raised his head after a moment's thought. 'Yeah, sort o' a notion, nothin' very real. I remember thinkin' there was somethin' goin' on out there in the darkness. Nothin' to see or hear . . . just a feelin'. Like someone waitin' . . . a danger, you know?'

'I can imagine, Billy. Welcome to *my* world. Tell me, did you ever threaten Chester Jarrow?'

'Hell no. I was plenty mad at him, though. It wasn't a big loan we asked for, just a couple o' hundred dollars. It was me called him a tight-wad, said he probably didn't chew baccy 'cause he'd have to spit. But it was no secret in town.'

'So everybody knew you were angry with him?'

'Me, yeah. The town an' their dogs, I reckon.'

The two men were silent for a while. Billy frowned across at Houston. 'What you thinkin' now?' he asked.

'A few things,' Houston replied. 'Like options.'

'How'd you mean?'

'Options. Other men. Other motives. Reasons why someone else would want to kill a bank president.'

Billy eyed Houston in puzzlement. 'I still don't understand.'

'It's one thing *you not* killing him, Billy. It's another pondering on *who did*. And why.'

'Are you sayin' you think maybe I didn't do it?'

107

'Not exactly. But maybe there's time to consider it,' Houston mused. 'Jarrow's deep in the bone-yard by now, I shouldn't wonder. And if it wasn't you, the real killer's hitting town somewhere . . . pouches swollen with spending cash.'

'Yeah, Cedar City most likely,' Billy growled. 'Leavin' me to pay for what they all did.'

'If they were strangers in Bullhead, how come they knew about your feelings for Jarrow . . . that you were a broke, irresponsible, swill-pot? How'd they know that, Billy?'

'Accordin' to Sheriff Games, most o' the county knew it.'

'Well, let's start by assuming you're *not* guilty,' Houston said. 'But your gun and a piece of your shirt *were*. They were there . . . found in the bank. Think hard now, Billy. You *were* sober when you arrived at Delano's . . . the saloon you took to do your watering at?'

'Cold sober. The only thing my gut was full o' was dust. But I didn't stay that way for long . . . that's for sure. But two drinks was all I had, Houston. Two lousy fingers o' cut-down corn.'

'Presumably you didn't go through the doors with an empty holster, and your shirt wasn't torn?'

' 'Course not.'

'You got to feeling weary, so you didn't leave . . . *couldn't* leave, and found your way to a back room and collapsed. How long do you reckon you were there before getting arrested?'

'I dunno. I was out of it . . . didn't wake till they stashed me in a cell.'

'You went on sleeping while they dragged you away from the saloon?' Huston asked incredulously.

'Must have. I sure can't recall anythin'.'

'You normally go like that after a bender?'

'Only when I'm drunk . . . if you know what I'm sayin'.'

'I think so. There was a window in that room you were in?' Houston asked.

'Yeah, there was a window.'

'And a back alley beyond?'

'Yeah, one o' them too.'

'So, you're saying you never woke, stirred even, when someone came off that alleyway, through the window and helped themselves to your Colt and a piece of shirt.'

Billy shook his head and cursed knowingly. 'Weren't too difficult, I guess. It's the only time it could've happened. But it ain't goin' to help any. Who'd believe *you* . . . with respect?'

'I'm trying to be reasonable, Billy. Thinking out loud more than anything. Trying to find answers.' Houston thought deeply for a long moment. 'Would you know what kind of safe it was?' he asked. 'The bank safe.'

'One for keepin' piles o' cash in, I suppose. I couldn't tell the difference between one o' them an' a tumbleweed. Why?'

'I just wondered . . . thinking out loud, again.'

109

Billy stared into the fire a while then lifted his head. 'You really startin' to believe I didn't do it?'

'Thinking about it and listening to you, it's getting harder to believe you did.'

'Much obliged. I'll tell the hangman that.' Billy spread his blanket and rolled into it. 'You're not really goin' to wake Pa, are you?' he added. 'You're goin' to watch me all night . . . just in case.'

'Whatever you're using for a brain, Billy, you should've used it long before now.'

Inside the wagon, Billy's mother moved about fitfully for half an hour, then, like Mimsy, lapsed into deeper sleep. Under the wagon, it wasn't long before Harve and Gramps broke the silence of night with their duet of snores.

Houston sat quiet and contemplative, occasionally dropping a branch on the fire. In the first, early hours, he brewed and drank two cans of coffee. Throughout the long darkness he pondered every aspect of the case, thinking back over Billy's story, looking for ambiguity, inconsistencies.

He was still sitting there when Mimsy climbed down from the wagon and came over to the fire. At first light he had heard sounds, the clank of a tin jug, splashing of water in a bowl. Mimsy's eyes were clear, her fair hair was pinned, coiled atop her head.

'I'll bet you've been awake all night,' she gently accused as she sat beside him. 'I'm not surprised, though. You didn't feel like trustin' Pa with Billy.'

'I saw it as not throwing temptation at either of them.'

'Hmm, you sure are the strangest man,' she frowned. 'An' you don't look at all tired for it.'

'Well I've been called a few things in my time, Mimsy, but I don't recall, *strange* and *not looking tired*, being among them. How about, *looking hungry*?'

'Ma's awake,' she said. 'Pa too. We'll start fixin' breakfast soon.' Mimsy looked across to where her brother lay, and her eyes filled with sadness. 'When he's like that, all that stuff about him seems unlikely.'

'Most of us look innocent enough when we're asleep, Mimsy,' Houston replied. 'Billy always been a good brother, has he?'

'Yes, mostly. Do you think he could have done such a terrible thing?'

'It's getting to seem more unlikely, I must admit. There's strong evidence against him though, and even if the deputy Levitch ain't up to much, he shouldn't have broken jail. But maybe any youngster in his position would have done the same. For Billy, I think they'd call it extenuating circumstances . . . not that anyone actually will.'

'But you're goin' to help him, Mr Houston?'

'I've sort of agreed to do what I can.' Houston gave the girl a reassuring grin, nodded towards Billy. 'Go ahead and wake him.'

Harve and Gramps were approaching the fire. They stopped to watch Mimsy kneel beside her

111

brother and shake his shoulder.

'Mornin', Sis,' Billy mumbled and opened his eyes. 'Some things never change.'

Harve looked to Houston. 'You were supposed to wake me, feller. Give me a turn at lookin' out.'

'Yeah, sorry. I guess I must have dozed off,' Houston replied. 'Now we've all managed some shut-eye.'

Billy sat up, rubbed his eyes and licked his lips. 'Goddamn jawbone. Let's eat an' move on . . . get it over with,' he said.

11

At mid-morning, Glim Savotta and Jack Carboys were approaching from the east, less than a mile from George Houston and the westbound Carricks. But they'd been riding easy, working on the assumption that even if their fugitive managed to reach the foothills, he'd be forced to linger there.

'Be as weak as a newborn,' Savotta sneered. 'If his legs hold him he'll head for his ol' man's diggin's.'

'Yeah, but only if he makes it out of the desert,' Carboys added. 'And with only one canteen, it don't seem likely.'

'We'll look over the west rim for a spell. Then we'll know for sure,' Savotta decided.

The trail wound its way to a higher bench and the two men could see many miles to the west. Moments after reining in, Savotta cursed. 'We're goin' back. Let's move,' he rasped angrily.

Carboys glanced westward, then hastily wheeled his mount and scampered after Savotta. They retreated a few hundred yards, came to where hunks of lava edged the trail. Savotta swung down, with his big hands, dragged his rifle from its sheath.

'Who are they?' Carboys wanted to know. 'You lit out like it was the boogerman himself.'

'Just get these horses behind the rocks,' Savotta snapped.

Carboys led the horses beyond the rock-mounds to conceal them and quickly fashioned close-hobbles, then he doubled back to join Savotta. 'Who the hell are they, Glim?' he asked again. 'Who the hell are we hidin' from?'

The stocky, erstwhile posse-man was prone beside one of the lava-mounds. 'It's one of 'em muleskinner wagons, but I don't know who's in it,' he replied. 'I don't recognize who's ridin' up with 'em either. But I spotted the two out front. One of 'em's Houston . . . the bounty hunter. Remember him . . . the one who sassed Dod at Land's bar? The other one's. . . .'

'Carrick,' Carboys gasped. 'Jeez, don't say it's him . . . Billy Carrick.'

'Yeah, it's him.' Savotta nodded. 'I couldn't be mistaken. He's still wearin' Dod's bonnet an' lookin' very alive.'

'No. It don't make sense,' Carboys protested.

'He must've found somethin' to drink,' Savotta said.

'How?' Carboys argued. 'Unless he did know of a couple of water holes.'

'Yeah, whatever.' Savotta nestled into a shooting position. 'But as of now, him an' the bounty hunter are headed right this way. Our job's to see it's as far as they get.'

'I guess it's got to be done . . . eh Glim?' For the shortest moment, Carboys hesitated, almost as though he had qualms.

'You remember what Dod said?' Savotta reminded him. 'If Billy Carrick's allowed to spout off in court, someone might get curious. He also said a dead suspect was usually a guilty one.'

'That was it, yeah. So what about the bounty hunter? We goin' to knock him off too? And the other folk? What about them?' Carboys fretted.

'Houston won't give up his fat payment without a fight. As for the others . . . that's up to them.'

'As long as they don't see us . . . our faces, anyway,' Carboys hoped.

'They don't have to get hurt if they keep out of it . . . whoever they are.'

'And if they decide to buy in?'

'We'll have to silence 'em . . . permanent. There's no choice. After takin' care of Houston, it'll be them or us. They're on the risin' ground now,' Savotta observed. 'We'll let 'em get a bit closer.'

If Savotta had had more time to set up his ambush, the outcomes might have been grave for Houston and Billy Carrick . . . maybe the whole Carrick family. After watching them descend the grade and move along a straggled line of stunt pine,

Savotta judged his intended victims to be well within rifle range. He selected the unsuspecting Billy and levelled his sights, muttered a short command to Carboys, and two rifles barked in unison.

Savotta was a better marksman, but his bullet failed to kill. It struck Billy's right shoulder with such impact that he was jerked from the saddle, thrown to the ground over his mount's rump. Jack Carboys' bullet had buzzed more than a foot somewhere to the left of Houston. At the sound of the rifles' reports, Houston had impulsively thrown himself from the saddle. But this time carefully landing on his feet, and instantly went into a crouch.

'Christ, not again,' he yelled. 'Who the hell is this sumbitch?' There was no time or need to warn Harve Carrick. The man had wheeled his mount, was shouting warnings to his father.

Gramps shoved the women back into the interior of the rig. He turned the team, was starting them on a lumbering run through a gap in the gnarled pine.

'Billy,' Harve yelled anxiously.

'Stay behind the trees and keep your heads down. I'll take care of the boy,' Houston shouted back.

Harve and Gramps were breaking out their assortment of weapons from the foot locker. From the edge of the timber, were using scrubby cover to

116

consider their retaliation.

Taking advantage of Savotta and Carboys having played their hand, being momentarily indecisive, Houston dashed to where Billy lay. He gripped the wounded youngster under the arms, stumbled backwards towards the trees.

'Shoulder wound,' he called out. 'We'll get him into the wagon. He won't die.'

'I figure there's a pair of 'em,' Gramps said.

'Yeah, two rifles. I've near spotted their position.' Houston pulled Billy closer, cursing as more bullets whined through the air and smacked into the timber, between its low branches. Mimsy clambered from the wagon, helped him to lift and drag Billy onto the wagon-bed. Speaking softly, Ma Carrick immediately started to unfasten the bloodied shirt.

'If you've got any kind of bug killer, pour some on the wound,' Houston told her. 'Don't worry about the bullet just yet. It's usually dirt from clothing that does the damage.'

'We've got a jug o' Gramps' shine,' Mimsy said.

Houston nodded. 'Yeah, that'll do. Whatever it is, I don't expect germs to like it too much.'

He ducked as he walked hurriedly from the rear of the wagon to where the Carrick men were crouched. Gramps grimaced as a rifle bullet puffed up the sandy dirt, another gouged bark and splinters from a low, pine trunk.

'They got plenty ammunition, goddamn 'em,' he

117

seethed. 'That an' a sense o' purpose is a deadly combination.'

'That's right, Gramps, but we got honour an' justice on our side,' Houston mocked a reply. 'While you two keep everyone busy, I'll try to get round the back of them. I can't think of a better way.'

'Maybe you can take 'em alive,' Harve suggested. 'If Jarrow's widow only offered bounty to *you*, I'm wonderin' on their sense o' purpose.'

'That's my thinking too,' Houston replied.

'Not as if there's a reward dodger out on Billy,' Harve continued.

'No. I'm just as interested as you are, Harve. Believe me.'

A few minutes later Houston was moving from the cover of the line of timber. He dodged and weaved between clumps of sagebrush, hugging all the cover he could, working his way around in a wide, half circle.

Besieged by the hand guns of Harve and the old man, the assailants didn't have much choice. They could retreat or stay put, trading shot for shot with the men hidden in the trees. Even if – as Gramps Carrick suspected – they did have a plentiful supply of bullets, their quarry could well have themselves a virtual ammunition wagon. For the time being they were staying on slightly higher ground. Moreover, Savotta had seen his victim fall, wanted to be certain he was dead.

Beyond sandstone rocks, Houston made another turn. He went to his hands and knees through taller grass and shadscale. There was actually little concealment, no resistance against lead from a brace of rifles. He crawled cautiously, silently prepared until he was within fifty feet of Savotta and Carboys at their vantage point. He rose to one knee, gripped the butt of his Colt in both hands.

'Stop firing. Stop right now.' His command was loud and clear.

Savotta froze a moment, but Carboys rolled over and away fast. He let go his rifle, clutched for his holstered Colt. He slewed around and swung his gun up towards Houston.

But Houston maintained the edge, was ahead of the game. He fired, and as the shot crashed out, Carboys gasped and shuddered, his Colt falling from his already lifeless fingers.

'I said to stop your firing,' Houston yelled. But Savotta thrust his rifle out in front of him and cracked off a shot. The bullet was way high and allowed Houston to fire once again. He hit Savotta in the top of the leg, thought it might end there. But it didn't and Savotta levered another round into the breech and raised the barrel to fire.

'Stupid. I got no goddamn choice,' Houston said, and in the interest of self-preservation, fired again.

Savotta's upper chest erupted into a dark-red bloom. With little further movement he slumped

119

forward, lay motionless amid the sandy dirt and thin black-brush.

Houston set himself straight, walked slowly towards the two bodies until it was obvious there was no further need for caution. Savotta had died with what appeared to be a curse warping his mouth. Carboys' eyes were wide open with hopelessness.

The bounty hunter eyed the massive sky. 'We're sort of in the same line of business,' he muttered to the distant vultures. 'And I'm not the burying type.' He looked down towards the trees, raised a hand high in the air.

Harve Carrick, who was considering a speculative shot, lowered his scattergun. 'That's Houston,' he said. 'He's on our side.'

'Yeah,' Gramps grunted. 'I reckon he'll have finished 'em.'

On his way back to the ribbon of gnarled pine, Houston reloaded his Colt with a full cylinder. 'You can go and take a look,' he said as Harve came running towards him. 'There's nothing to be done, except perhaps put a name to them. But your Billy's got a bullet needs digging out.'

'We don't have medical stuff,' Harve fretted. 'Just more o' Gramps' firewater.'

'Then it'll hurt some,' Houston replied. 'Get a fire going and I'll need a sharp knife. Ask the ladies for some strips of bandage. We'll manage.'

'Are them bush-whackers dead?' Gramps asked,

120

earnestly gripping his big Patterson Colt.

'Yeah. You were right about being two of them, and they didn't give me any choice. Now I've got to do some doctoring.'

12

There was no panic, no shows of emotion during Houston's basic, bloody removal of the bullet from Billy's shoulder. Ma Carrick waved away the flies and generally remained stoic. Mimsy stood beside Houston, ready to hand him the items he needed, such as they were. Gramps kept the fire going and Harve honed the long blade of their skinner on a flat stone.

An examination of the wound revealed a rifle slug lodged in the top flesh of Billy's right shoulder. For probing, Houston used the tip of the slim-bladed knife, having sterilized it in a can of boiling water. The slug came out, and Houston had a close look at it before tossing it aside. For ten minutes, Billy endured unquestionable suffering with quieter reserve than Houston had expected.

When the basic surgical treatment was finished, the wound was soused with more of Gramps' moonshine, bound securely with strips torn from clean under-linen.

'Where'd you learn to do that?' Gramps asked.

'Knoxville '63,' Houston said. 'General Newton's horse caught a grey-back bullet and someone had to save it. I had the steadiest hands.'

Mimsy attended to a coffee brew while Gramps held his jug up to his ear and shook it. 'Soon be down to my last twenty or so jugs,' he muttered mischievously. 'Reckon we've all earned ourselves a likkerin'.'

'Count me in, Gramps. Don't want to waste it on any goddamn shoulder,' Billy spoke with a subdued voice. 'I hurt like hell an' you're responsible,' he added, staring up at Houston.

'Yeah, but it's not half as bad as I *could* have made it,' Houston replied. 'You'll be weak for a while from losing blood and you'll carry a memorable scar. Such is life, eh kid?'

Ma Carrick gave Houston a friendly grin. 'You sure take good care o' your captives, I'll say that for you,' she said.

'Thank you, ma'am. I'll wager what you're really thinking is, it's someone looking to their assets.' Houston looked at Harve. 'You recognize any of that bad meat?' he asked.

'Maybe,' Harve replied. 'Maybe I've seen 'em in town. No reason to keep 'em in mind.'

'Yellow-bellied scum suckers could be a name for 'em,' Billy seethed.

'Stay quiet, son . . . don't want the blood to start runnin',' his ma chided.

'Yeah, do as your ma says,' Houston furthered. 'I'm going to take a look at the scum, before the vultures get to 'em. I'll be back for coffee.'

Unhurriedly, Houston made his way back to the rising rock. Before looking at the bodies of the two riflemen, he looked for and found their hobbled horses. In the saddle pouches he found cheap whiskey and basic foodstuff but nothing to identify their owners. He led the animals back, then spent a few moments looking down at the stiff faces of the dead men. Glim Savotta he remembered. He had seen him arriving with Myron Games' deputy at the Land Hotel bar on the night of his tussle with the belligerent blacksmith. He couldn't place Jack Carboys, but recognizing Savotta was enough to piqué his concern.

Neither man was carrying much money. Savotta had some coin, fifteen dollars in notes. The other man's fund was similarly thin. There were the other usual items of tobacco sacks, matches, pocketknife etc. But then Houston found the small, waxed-paper packets, one in Savotta's shirt pocket, the other in Carboys' coat pocket. If he hadn't been searching so thoroughly, he might easily have overlooked them. He unfolded one of the packages and contemplated the broken pills. But, hearing someone approach he flipped the packets closed and tucked them in his pants pocket.

Without taking his eyes off Savotta and Carboys, Harve Carrick walked straight up to Houston. 'What do we do with 'em ... Billy's scum?' he asked. 'Should we take 'em to town. Sheriff's got to be told.'

'You inform the sheriff every time you find a couple of dead men, do you?' Houston asked. 'Don't answer that. Just help me tie them to their horses. I want Billy to take a look at them.'

'You think he knew 'em?'

'He's spent more time in Bullhead than any other one of you, apparently ... hasn't he? So he might.'

'OK,' Harve said. 'Have you figured out why they ambushed us?'

'No, I haven't.' Houston looked to where fresh campfire smoke drifted upwards. 'There's a *few things* I haven't figured out yet.'

'Well I'll tell you somethin' I have,' Harve started. 'Robbin' a bank's one thing, pistol whippin' Chester Jarrow to death's somethin' else. My Billy couldn't do it, drunk or sober.'

'I agree,' Houston said. 'But proving it's going to be a problem.'

The corpses were folded across the horses' backs. They were lashed securely and Harve led them to the edge of the line of timber.

Ignoring the worried protests of his mother and sister, Billy was struggling to his feet. He made it, but was unsteady when Houston reached him.

'Well done, kid . . . in a state you're probably more used to,' Houston jibed. 'It'll be the Carrick grog that's giving you trouble. The shoulder's just pain, but you're a tough bumpkin. Can you walk aways?'

'Just point to where,' Billy replied. 'Take more'n one bullet to lay me up.'

'We all know what does *that*, Billy,' Mimsy contributed, a bit stingingly.

'They're a real laugh, ain't they?' Gramps added.

'I want these bodies looked at,' Houston said. 'Could be they're not total strangers.'

'Well they sure ain't friends,' Billy said as they set off slowly through the gnarled pines.

Minutes later, Harve scowled with disgust, cursed under his breath as Houston grabbed hold of a shirt collar and lifted a dead face. Leaning in slightly, Billy studied the ashen features of Savotta and Carboys, but without any immediate response.

'Well, unless they got more than one face apiece, that's it,' Houston said. 'Do you recognize them?'

'The stocky one. His name's Savotta . . . Glim Savotta,' Billy said. 'He ran a stump farm a few miles out from Bullhead. I don't know the other one, but he worked for Savotta.'

'Was this Savotta a friend of the deputy . . . Levitch?'

'I seen 'em drinkin' together. I guess he knew him well enough,' Billy mused.

'All right,' Houston said. 'Let's go get some of

126

that coffee.'

By the time they got back to the campfire, Billy was regretting his eagerness to recover. Pallid and spent, he sagged to his knees while his ma draped a blanket across his shoulders. Mimsy poured coffee and Gramps poured his raw whiskey into four of the cans.

To the dismay of his family, Billy proposed a bleak toast. 'Here's to a short, happy life . . . mine,' he muttered.

'You shouldn't talk that way, Billy,' his sister said.

'Why not? You think I should pretend we're goin' to my majority stomp?'

'You don't want to give up hope just yet,' Houston contributed.

The Carricks became silent. They eyed him in anticipation of something further, and Billy picked up on it.

'Are you still sayin' there's a chance?' he asked.

'I'm saying there's one or two things cropped up could possibly prove you're not guilty,' Houston replied. 'But it means me figuring them out.'

'What things?' Harve prodded.

'When I started out to find Billy, someone tried to kill me. Why? What was it to them?'

'You said one or two things. What else?' Gramps wanted to know.

'Why did we get bush-whacked by that brace of turkeys? Are the two connected?'

'Well, they ain't ever goin' to tell you,' Billy said.

'No. That's for them to have known, and me to find out,' Houston muttered. He took a few sips at his laced coffee, stared hard at Billy. 'The night it happened, you went to that saloon, had two short drinks . . . just two, and started to lose your grip . . . went dopey?'

'Yeah. That's about what happened,' Billy frowned.

'And I'm thinking I know why,' Houston said, more to himself than anyone else. 'Were Savotta and the other one there . . . anywhere near you?'

'Yeah. There was the three of 'em.'

'Three?'

'Fats Denvy. Funny thing, I never had him pegged as a ranchin' man. He's supposed to be one though.'

Houston thought for a moment. 'Did you sit at a table or were you standing at the bar?'

'Delano's ain't the sort o' place you want to sit down. Besides, an' like I said, I weren't for stayin' long.'

'So they were close by?'

'Yeah. You're always up close to someone in that place.' Billy scratched his head. 'Denvy had a curious, clean kind o' whiff about him, I remember.'

'That's about the time your head started to spin? Whether you knew it or not, you went into a back room, passed out and didn't wake till you were in jail?'

'I already told you. Why do I have to keep sayin' it over an' over?'

Houston lowered his head, raised his eyes and gave Billy a meaningful look. 'Because, now it means something different to when you first said it. It could be real important.'

Everyone sat quietly for a while, mostly wondering what it was that might be important. Houston did some figuring while the Carrick family continued to watch and wait. He recalled the night of his run-in with the blacksmith, how soon afterwards the posse returned and Deputy Levitch gave his account to Myron Games of the wild goose chase they'd been on. And Glim Savotta – the man who thought little of ambushing an unarmed man – had been with him.

'This Savotta must have been real wound-up . . . desperate about something,' he suggested.

'What the hell about?' Harve protested. 'He could see Billy was your prisoner an' that you were ridin' to Bullhead. Why'd he want to kill him?'

'Interesting question,' Houston said. He moved away from the fire, sat with his back against the gnarled bole of a pine. 'Tell me again,' he directed at Billy. 'Tell me about your escape . . . how it happened. Don't leave out anything, and start from where Levitch came into the cell and talked to you.'

'What's the use?'

'Listen, it's small peas to me whether you're guilty or innocent,' Houston snorted back. 'I'm being paid to bring you in. Any feeling I've got for justice is getting more to do with your folk than you. *That's* the goddamn use of it. So, tell me again.'

Billy scowled ineffectively, started to recount the story of his break from the Bullhead jail. Now and again, Houston interrupted to clarify and picture elements of the incident.

'Levitch actually turned away from you? You got to his gun by just reaching through the bars?' he questioned. 'Hell, there's a sign in most law offices saying no guns be taken into the cells.'

'Yeah, well there's probably one there too. Didn't seem to trouble the deputy.'

'And what was it you heard in the back yard?'

Billy considered thoughtfully. 'It was more o' a feelin' that somethin' was out there. Somethin' in the darkness.'

'So you backed off . . . stole Levitch's hat and coat and horse?'

'That's about the order of it. I wasn't goin' to stay, an' you know the rest.'

'It's like understanding the bits of a jigsaw. We've got them all, just got to fit them together. Keep talking anyway,' Houston said.

Billy continued, describing best he could, his journey into and across the scorched wasteland, why he had to kill the deputy's bay mare. 'It fell . . . threw me when we were movin' down the bench an' broke its leg. Only thing I could do was put it out of its misery.'

130

'I wondered why you didn't shoot it,' Houston said. 'You weren't to know I was close behind you, and you had a gun . . . Levitch's. It wouldn't have been so up close and personal.'

'I did . . . or tried to. The goddamn Colt wouldn't work . . . was just a pretty fake. But he had a sheath-knife as well. Huh. Hell of a thing to do.'

'Yeah, I can imagine. Why didn't Levitch's gun fire?'

'It just wouldn't. I checked it . . . reloaded it from the belt. Useless as tits on a bull.'

Slowly, Houston got to his feet. Harve and Gramps growled out some questions, but he didn't answer. From his saddlebag he produced the hol-stered Colt he had taken from Billy. He checked the cylinder, actioned it, pointed the barrel to the sky and squeezed the trigger. Nothing happened, and he repeated the action.

'Take my word for it,' Billy said, 'Levitch had himself a fancy-dress piece.'

'I don't think he did,' Houston said, turning to Gramps. 'You seen a few things in your time,' he continued, 'so take a look at this.'

The Carrick elder removed the cylinder from Levitch's Colt, took a quick look and worked the action. 'Nothin' here that a decent chamber of ammo won't take care of,' he said. 'Fancy, don't mean no good.'

Houston agreed. '*Somebody* was making sure Billy didn't shoot somebody else,' he said. 'If the Colt

131

had been empty, he would have noticed immediately . . . maybe on a single cartridge. So, every cartridge had to have been tampered with.'

'Lookin' like Levitch *wanted* Billy to make a run for it,' Gramps wryly suggested.

'Yeah, straight into who or whatever was out there in the dark waitin',' Billy speculated eagerly. 'I was right.'

'You were a prisoner being held on a murder charge, not tinhorn pilfering,' Houston pointed out, sharply. 'It could have been Games' legit set-up. But I doubt it.'

'Levitch said I'd never make it,' Billy recalled.

'He was warning you off,' Houston reasoned. 'He meant you to head out the back way . . . get cut down with a useless gun in your hand. Shot while trying to escape's always been a favourite of bad lawmen.'

'Why the hell would a deputy sheriff do that?' Harve wondered. 'They were all so goddamn sure Billy was guilty . . . so sure he'd hang. Why'd they want to push it like that?'

'There's probably a reason why Levitch wanted the affair closed down. The storm wiped out tracks of the other men, and Billy was the only one taken in. Evidence said it was him did the killing while the safe was emptied. A convenient ending was Billy getting shot dead. There'd have been no need for further investigation.'

'Neat as a pin,' Harve agreed.

'When Billy decided to leave by the front door, the plan was spoiled,' Houston continued. 'But he tracked Billy until he was sure where he was headed, then figured he'd die anyway. He started worrying again when he learned I was going after Billy with supplies and water.'

'You reckon?' Harve asked.

'Yeah, unless you got another, better idea,' Houston countered. 'Mine's the only one I got.'

'You reckon Levitch was the one who took a shot at you at the creek?' Billy demanded.

Houston nodded. 'Him or Savotta. Levitch couldn't afford for me to find you. He could have guessed easy where I was headed.'

'Guesses an' ideas ain't much use where Billy's headed,' Harve fretted.

'That's my problem,' Houston agreed. 'I've got something to do. Savotta and his partner will have to be kept out of sight. So, if there's a shovel in the wagon. . ..?'

'You're not servin' 'em up to Sheriff Games, then?' Gramps asked.

'No. Levitch might be with him.'

'Sounds like Dod Levitch's future has got as much prospect as mine had,' Billy huffed.

'The law don't take to one of its own going bad,' Houston said. He got to his feet, moved away from the fire and stared south. A couple hundred yards from the trail he could see high mesquite, beyond which started the foothills of the Black Mountains.

133

'Somewhere out there's fine,' he suggested and pointed.

'For what?' Harve asked.

'The next Carrick camp. It'll give your boy a chance to get some strength back into him.'

'I . . . we thought you were takin' him. An' I couldn't let you do that,' Harve said.

'I won't be taking Billy into town. I knew you'd say something like that and I didn't want to put you in such a corner,' Houston proposed. 'I'll take his bloody shirt instead. It don't mean a thing of course, but it'll help the eyes of their minds.'

'He stays here?' Ma asked hopefully.

'Yes. Instead, I want to take Mimsy. It's a big ask I know . . . the biggest. But right now, it's the best way to help I can think of.'

'How can the girl help?' the girl's ma demanded.

'Because she's interested in acting,' Houston said and looked towards Mimsy. 'And in Bullhead right now, there's boards just waiting to be trodden on.'

'I don't understand,' Mimsy joined in.

'You will,' Houston promised. 'I'll explain while we're riding. It'll be a matinee performance.'

'You've got to make it all a lot plainer before Mimsy rides anywhere with you, mister,' Harve warned.

'OK. The way I see it, Levitch has got to be tricked into a wrong move. Let him think he's succeeded . . . that it's over and there's no more risk. I reckon Miss Mimsy can help.' Houston continued

134

to explain, but his small audience met his plan with little conviction.

'I know. But this side of shooting Levitch, what else is there?' he asked.

From Mimsy there was a spark of keenness. 'I can do it,' she declared. 'I can try, for Billy.'

'Thanks, Sis. You always were good at puttin' it on,' Billy said. 'Just don't overdo it.'

'That'll be difficult,' Houston added. 'Any girl would be near hysterical with seeing her brother killed.' He eyed Harve and Ma solemnly. 'I'll take good care of her, Mrs Carrick. You can't suddenly stop trusting me.'

Gramps voiced his assurance. 'I reckon he's levellin' with us,' he said. 'I reckon he'll do right by Mimsy. He has all o' us so far. Billy would likely be dead twice over if it wasn't for him. Besides, the kid knows how to look after herself.'

'All right, Mr Houston,' Harve conceded. 'But remember, she's our daughter.'

'If you ride now, you can reach Bullhead early tomorrow afternoon. You'll get no more'n a couple o' hours sleep tonight, though,' Billy said.

'There'll come a time when I catch up on that,' Houston replied. 'My eagerness – if that's the right word – is about as palpable as yours. I can still sense that bullet thumping past my neck.'

'Just remember what Pa said about our Mimsy,' Billy concluded. 'She ain't anyone's bait.'

13

Mid-afternoon the following day, Dod Levitch walked out of Bullhead's telegraph office. Ahead of him along the main street, Myron Games was sitting quietly on the porch outside of the jailhouse. His left leg was resting on the low rail of the balustrade.

'No news, I bet,' he said as Levitch approached.

The deputy shook his head. 'No, nothin'. I did like you said an' wired every lawman for as far as they could have ridden ... even further. Seems there's been no riders spendin' big. Whoever robbed the bank's keepin' their purse strings well drawn.'

'There's no one in Bullhead will ever see that money again ... Billy Carrick neither,' Games sighed.

'At least you know Chester's killer got what was comin' to him. It's some consolation,' Levitch said.

'I don't get much consolation from that, Dod. And it's none for Mrs Jarrow.' The sheriff's piercing blue eyes narrowed as he squinted along the main street. 'I'm wonderin' about the bounty killer . . . Houston. What happened to him?'

'He could be dead too,' Levitch suggested. 'It makes some sort o' sense.'

'I don't know,' Games pondered. 'If he was totin' plenty water an' fixin's, it's possible he could've reached the boy in time. It ain't *impossible*.' He shrugged forlornly. 'If Houston *had* found him, he'd have been back in town by now.'

A half hour later, Houston and Mimsy Carrick arrived at the outskirts of Bullhead. They rode in from the west, quietly and steadily to near the middle of town. Houston wasn't ready to show himself anywhere on, or even close to the main street, but he *was* looking to have a few words with Orville Land.

'You wait right here, and I mean right here, Mimsy,' he said, as they reined up in the lane behind the hotel. If anybody gets curious while I'm in there, you know what to say. I won't be more than a minute or two, then we'll go see the sheriff and you'll get your walk-on part.'

'Scene one, act one,' Mimsy answered and smiled. 'I'm ready if you are.'

Houston dismounted, walked quickly across the hotel's back yard to the rear door. Someone gave him a careless glance as he moved through the kitchen area to the lobby, but said nothing. The front area of the hotel was deserted, except for Land who was writing mechanically on a pad of foolscap.

'Make sure the name's spelled right,' he said.

Land stopped writing and looked up. He brushed the side of his big nose with his hand, grinned a greeting. 'Mr Houston. Glad to see you back . . . safely. Did you find what you were after?'

'I'll tell you later.' Houston got closer, flicked a glance towards the entrance. 'Right now, I'm in need of your help.'

'Certainly. That is, if I can be. . . .

'Well if you can, I'll make it worth your time.'

'I take it you're not talking money?'

'No. Your currency . . . sort of. A fat chapter written as an eyewitness and as it happens. What do you say?'

'What do you want me to do?' Land replied promptly.

Houston dropped his voice. 'Chances are I'm getting to the nub of the Jarrow killing and the whereabouts of all those dollars. You could be with the story . . . the whole story, just by using your eyes and ears.'

'Yes. So, tell me,' Land said.

'I want you to keep an eye on the deputy sheriff.'

'Dod Levitch?'

'Yeah, him. He's going to leave town shortly, and when he does, I want to know where he's headed. When you're sure of the route he's taking, come back and tell me. I'll be with Games at the law office. Do you reckon you can do that? There's not a heap of folk I can ask, you'll appreciate.'

'I can manage it,' Land affirmed. 'You think he's involved?'

'My thinking's no more than that,' Houston countered. 'At the moment I'm just riding with a gut feeling. But there's a story waiting ... and it won't be fiction. Not unless you're tooling up with a six-shooter as the dime-novel hero. That bit don't matter to me.'

'Well it does to me, Mr Houston. Heroes are usually brave for just a few minutes longer. I'm looking for something more long-term. As for our deputy, I did see him a short while ago. He was out on the law office porch, talking to Games.'

Houston nodded. 'Good. That's where I'm off to now. Unless I'm making a big mistake, Levitch won't be staying around. That's when you join the party. Just don't let him see you.'

'I won't. Me and saddles don't have natural rapport, so I've got a buggy to get ready.'

'Whatever's normal,' Houston showed Land a tight but friendly enough grin, walked back towards the kitchen and the way out.

'All set. Now we can ride through to the main street,' he said, taking back the reins of the charcoal mare from Mimsy.

'And then I get to play the part?' she asked eagerly.

139

'Yeah. But not just in the street, remember. There's an audience. Small but significant. You reckon you can do it? Cry those tears?'

'I've done it before,' Mimsy assured. 'I could always start a blubber to fool Pa or Billy . . . sometimes even Ma.'

'OK. Right now you only got to fool Deputy Levitch. Let's go.'

They walked their horses along the side alley and into the main street. As they made their way to the law office, people on the sidewalk slowed, paused to eye them with curiosity. Mimsy rode slump-shouldered, started her sobbing act and Houston was suitably considerate. Only once, and under his breath did he have to advise restraint.

On the law office porch, Myron Games sat stiffly upright. Even at a distance, Houston could see Levitch was struggling to control his feelings, uncertain how to play the hand he knew was about to be dealt him. And there was no doubt in Houston's mind now as to the identity of the man who had taken a shot at him as he attempted to cross the creek. *Won't be long now, you son-of-a-bitch*, he thought with a feeling that verged on satisfaction.

Levitch's black Stetson was hung on Houston's saddle horn. He detached it as he reined in by the steps, tossed it casually up to the deputy.

'Not the sort of headgear you'd want to lose forever. I was told it's yours,' he said flatly.

140

'Yeah that's mine ... no mistake,' Levitch answered with a return of the coolness.

'I can't do the same for your Colt,' Houston continued. 'Carrick says it fell in a gopher hole.'

'You caught up with him?' Games demanded. The sheriff laboured up from his deck chair, gained some balance and looked hard towards Mimsy. 'Does she have to be here?'

'No, she doesn't, but I said she could ride along,' Houston responded. 'It's hard seeing your brother shot down in cold blood.'

'*You* shot him?'

'No, I didn't.' Houston shook his head, noticed inquisitive locals were drawing closer, bending their route for a sense of the home excitement. 'I caught up with him in the desert. We had a few words, then rode to his father's cabin for fresh horses.'

'An' he didn't try an' stop you?' Levitch interjected. 'That ol' goat shoots at anythin' ain't called Carrick.'

Houston shook his head. 'The boy's family all wanted him to come back and stand trial. Young Billy didn't take kindly to the idea, of course, but we didn't give him much choice. When we started back along the Bullhead trail, Miss Mimsy insisted on riding with us. I didn't want to get ambushed again and she said she knows the lay of the land as well as anyone.'

'As well as any goddamn coyote,' Levitch muttered.

141

'What's this about an ambush?' Games asked.

'Twice,' Houston corrected. 'At the creek before going into that wasteland after Carrick. Someone took a shot at me and I played fish . . . dead fish.'

'You didn't get a look at him then?' Levitch asked the heavy question.

'Another no.' Houston frowned, tried to keep his emotions in check. 'He was too far away.'

'If you weren't hit, why the hell didn't you chase him down? That sort of thing could be a real hindrance to one's career. A man like you,' Games wondered aloud.

'That's what I thought, but I wanted to find Carrick.' Houston stopped short of flicking a look at Levitch as he spoke. 'Besides, I knew there'd be some other time.'

'Come inside,' Games said, limping awkwardly to the office door. 'I want to know eveythin' that happened. Dod, look to the girl. She comes too.'

Houston swung down, unfastened his saddlebag and took out Billy Carrick's raggedy, blood-stained shirt. Mimsy stared at it, immediately choked, shook her head in distress.

'Sorry, Mimsy. I made a mistake,' Houston acknowledged. 'And I'm sure there'll be a few more before the day's done. You best get used to it.'

Anxiously, Levitch watched as Mimsy dismounted, followed her up the steps after Games and Houston.

'Put the goddamn wood in the hole,' Games

rasped when they were all inside. 'Those gawpin' towners have seen an' heard enough.' He lowered himself into his chair and Mimsy sat miserably on the office couch.

Levitch stood with his back to the door. It looked like he was blocking the route for anyone trying to escape, but Houston knew it was only the appearance. The deputy was tense, but he was covering his emotions.

'Miss Mimsy wanted to head for home, but she's a witness,' Houston said and dropped the remains of Billy's shirt onto the sheriff's desk. Games stared hard then frowned.

'Carrick's shirt,' he said, simply.

'Yeah,' Houston said. 'It don't prove anything . . . just about the most of what's left of him.'

'What the hell happened?' Games asked.

'They're gunshot wounds, for chris'sakes!' Houston snapped back. 'We were ambushed. Two turkeys with rifles blew him clear of the saddle.'

'And?' Levitch pitched in.

'I got angry and *they* got dead.'

Games smirked icily. 'But you didn't fetch in the bodies. Hell, you should have, an' you know it,' he rasped.

'In this heat?' Houston answered. 'As far as I'm concerned there's no point. I buried them with Carrick, and I'll take whatever rate this county's paying for burials.'

'Did they talk before they died?' Games pursued.

'Not the way I shot them, no.' Houston returned the chilly expression.

'So, did you recognize 'em?' Levitch tried to keep his voice unworried and unfussed.

'One of them could have been familiar. But that's about all. No time or place.'

'How about Carrick?' Games wanted to know. 'Didn't he tell you anythin' about where the loot was? No mention of it?'

'Of course he didn't say. Why the hell would he?' Houston returned. 'I don't think it was uppermost in his mind when I found him. He was hardly strong enough to stand. Later, when we changed horses at the Carrick place, he was stronger, but he kept his mouth shut. All he kept saying was, was that he was gallows bait. Huh, I guess that's the part he got right. He got tired of denying that he'd killed Jarrow . . . tired of everything at the end.'

'My brother Billy wasn't a murderer,' Mimsy sobbed. 'An' he wouldn't steal for his supper, even.'

'OK, girl, it's too bad you had to see it happen,' Games replied. 'But like Houston's already told you, cryin' an' protestin' ain't goin' to make it any easier.' The sheriff switched his attention to his deputy. 'Well Dod, I guess that's just about the end of all this.'

For a short moment Levitch didn't respond. 'Yeah,' he faltered as though in reserve about the sheriff's deliberation. 'Yeah, looks like it.'

'The end of the action anyways. There's still

some whys an' wherefores, eh Houston . . . some unanswered questions?' Games said as though leading Houston.

'What's your thinking, Sheriff?'

'I'm wonderin' if those turkeys you met up with were those who helped Carrick crack the bank. Surely you searched 'em?'

Houston took money from his pocket and tossed it onto the desk. 'There's about forty dollars there. Nothing in their traps was worth a sous. They were without identity of any sort. That's how I buried them . . . with their guns.'

'An' where was that?' an increasingly thoughtful-looking Levitch demanded.

'Somewhere too good for them. About five miles back you can see a big curve in the mesquite. Beyond it's the foothills . . . a good view of the trees. They're fifty yards off the trail, not too deep down if you want to pay a visit,' Houston said.

'I know where it is,' Levitch said.

'Good, I reckon we ought . . .' Games started.

'Yeah, I know what you're goin' to say,' the deputy interrupted.

'We've got to make an effort to identify those bush-whackers,' Games advised. 'It shouldn't be too difficult . . . nothin's settled down yet. But don't forget to take a shovel.'

'I'll get goin',' Levitch nodded.

To Houston's way of thinking, Levitch's ready acceptance of such an offensive task was out of character. But it also carried a hint of relief.

Levitch was gone within moments. Games was going to say something more, but Houston moved to the front window and silenced him with a curt gesture.

'Give him a minute or two, Mimsy,' he said. 'Then you can get what's in my saddle-bag.'

Mimsy coughed lightly and got to her feet. Games' jaw dropped a fraction.

'What are you two up to?' he grated.

'It's the end of act one,' Mimsy said, almost smiled as she walked to the door.

'What the hell's goin' on, Houston? Where's she goin'?'

'The MD you got here in Bullhead. Does he know much about pills and stuff? You know, what's in them,' Houston asked by way of an answer.

'Doc Milford? He knows more'n most. Makes his own, I think . . . those he don't, get shipped in from Chicago. What do you want to know for?'

'I've got reasons,' Houston said.

Mimsy came back. She was carrying Levitch's holstered Colt and gun belt, was obviously still of lighter frame of mind. She handed the goods to Houston who was taking the small, waxed-paper packets from his pocket.

'Sheriff says it's Doc Milford who can help us,' he said, pressing one of them into her hand. 'His daytime surgery's along the street. Tell him what we want to know, that we want him back here to give us

146

his opinion.'

Houston then laid the gun and belt alongside Carrick's bloodied shirt.

'That's Dod's gun,' Games exclaimed. 'You said you buried 'em.'

'I know. I also said a few other things in front of your deputy that weren't exactly factual,' Houston replied. 'Take a look at the cartridges here. You'll find every one's been tampered with. This Colt's about as lethal as spit.'

'What are you talkin' about, Houston? Why the hell should Levitch's gun be duped?'

'Because he meant Billy Carrick to make a grab for it. He also meant him to escape through the back door. That was where his men would have shot him down like a rabid dog.'

'Keep talkin',' Games said. 'I ain't captured but I'm listenin'.'

'Billy Carrick's not dead. His family were helping bring him back for trial. We were ambushed, and Billy stopped a bullet. I dealt with them.'

'Yeah, so you said. The brace of turkeys you didn't recognize,' Games offered.

'That was for Levitch's benefit. One of them was familiar. Billy said his name was Glim Savotta. He also said Savotta was an associate of Levitch's.'

'What did the other one look like?'

Houston described the second gunman and Games nodded in recognition. 'Jack Carboys,' he said. 'The three of 'em worked a greasy sack spread

147

a few miles out of town.'

'Wasn't it Savotta who claimed it was three riders hightailed it away from the bank?' Houston asked.

'Yeah, Savotta,' Games confirmed. 'The riders who never were. Hell, that's why there's been no response to Levitch's wires. Huh, if he ever sent 'em. If I go with you on this, Houston, you explain Carrick's gun . . . the chunk of his shirt.'

'Very soon I think I'll be able to tell you how the whole thing was set up.'

'When Mimsy Carrick and the doc get here?'

'That's right. If Billy Carrick killed Chester Jarrow, my name really isn't George Houston.'

Games went quiet, fidgeted uncomfortably then cursed. 'No lawman wants to hear his deputy's corrupt . . . crooked,' he rasped with quiet anger. 'The son-of-a-bitch pinned on his star two years back an' I never had any reason to question him.'

'Well, how long does it take to go bad?' Houston asked. 'You can't ignore the cartridges. When Levitch went into that cell, he was inviting Billy to make a break. If Billy had gone through the back door, he'd have met Savotta, Carboys and Denvy. Met them with something less useful than a pea-shooter.'

'If Carrick had been killed durin' a break-out, there wouldn't be any case to answer . . . no need for a trial,' Games said.

'Yeah, what Levitch wanted,' Houston agreed. 'If not, he'd have been in real trouble. If Billy was ever

148

allowed to say his piece, the truth would have at least been heard ... maybe considered. No way Levitch could risk that.'

'*I* heard it, goddamnit,' Games scowled.

'You were too close. It needed an outside eye,' Houston persisted. 'Levitch would have been worried sick at Billy's escape. Maybe recovered a tad when he realized Billy had run to the desert with hardly any water. He found out I'd gone after Billy with a good chance I'd find him, so he had to stop *me*.'

'You're sayin' it was Dod out at the creek?'

'He's my best guess.'

'But Savotta an' Carboys were layin' for you else-where,' Games said with fitting surprise.

'Yeah.' Houston thought for a moment. 'Do you remember when you last saw them?'

'When they rode out with Dod ... after Carrick broke jail. I didn't see 'em after that, though.'

'They took the regular trail,' Houston suggested. 'They were all nervous about Billy. It didn't seem likely he'd get across that wasteland alive, but they had to be sure. They headed for the hills, in case he did.'

Games cursed quietly. He sliced his Brown Mule, popped a chaw into the side of his mouth. 'I'll wait for the girl an' her second act,' he said flatly, without humour.

Ten minutes later, Mimsy returned with Doc Milford. Games introduced Houston.

Milford nodded. 'Yes, I know who you are,' he said. 'I was in the hotel when you met up with Cuff Marteau.' The Bullhead MD placed a wax-packet on the desk-top and squinted at its contents. 'Yours, I believe?'

'No, not mine. And I'm not sure what it is either? A sedative?' Houston asked.

The doctor grinned, shook his head. 'It's some sort of horse-pill. I'd never administer a sedative that strong to a human. Don't reckon any other reputable MD would either. Too dangerous if the patient had any weaknesses.'

'Say he didn't. Say he was young, strong and healthy. What then?'

'If his heart stood up to it, he'd feel as though he'd been kicked and trampled by a mule team.'

'Sleep awhile then? On top of a drink or two.'

'Certainly. It wouldn't take many.'

'And when he came to, he'd have one hell of a headache?'

'He'd still be able to think and move around a bit. None of it too well, though. Where on earth did you get this?'

'Someone's pocket,' Houston said sharply. 'Doc, you've just explained how young Billy Carrick said he felt.'

'I recall him sayin' his head was fit to bust,' Games put in.

'Yeah, it's what he told me and anybody who'd listen,' Houston said. 'A couple of dust-settlers was all he could pay for. These are tablets I found on Savotta. Carboys had the others. But there was three of them together in the saloon, and it wasn't for their personal use. It was for Billy. Whoever got close enough to him.'

'Close enough to slip it into his drink,' Games concluded. 'Like a mickey finn.'

'Exactly.'

'They never came from any store or doctor's bag, believe me.' Milford frowned.

'I never thought they did,' Houston said. 'Billy reckons this Denvy character wasn't a regular of the Delano Saloon. He appeared to be more of a professional man . . . like yourself, Doc.'

'Hmm, I hope not. There's more than one sense to pushing pills,' Milford muttered. 'I hope my observations have been of help, gentleman. If that's all . . .'

'Yes, Doc, thanks. I'd guessed it, just wanted to know what you thought,' Houston said. 'If there's a fee, I'm sure the sheriff's office will oblige.'

When Doc Milford had gone, Houston looked at Games, keenly. 'It didn't have to be some sort of monkey that climbed into that back room while Billy was only half-conscious. It would have been easy for Levitch or any of his sidekicks,' he said, without trace of a smile or smirk.

'Yeah, any one of 'em,' Games agreed. 'Natural like. They tore a piece off his shirt an' stole his gun . . . took it all to the bank.' The sheriff turned to

151

Mimsy. 'Can I ask you to do somethin' now?' he asked. 'Ask the stableman to prepare a rig for me?' Turning to Houston he added, 'I have to bring in my deputy.'

'I know you do. But you won't be going alone,' Houston assured him. 'And you won't be looking for fresh-dug holes in the ground, either. You know where to go afterwards, Mimsy.'

'Yep, the hotel,' Mimsy nodded. 'I lock myself in your room an' wait for you to come fetch me.'

'That's it . . . act two,' Houston agreed and winked. 'Soon as this thing's over and done with, we'll ride back to your folks.'

'You should've been a lawman, Houston,' Games said after Mimsy had gone. 'Or a fisherman or a trapper.' He struggled up, made a pained face and let his crutches fall back to rest against the chair. 'Funny how stuff gets mended when there's sheriffin' to do,' he declared. 'Let's go see a man.'

'I'm sure of where he's gone,' Houston told him. 'We'll know as soon as . . .' He stopped what he was going to say because Orville Land was hauling in at the law office hitchrail. The hotel owner's face was flushed and beaded with sweat as he swung down to the street. He stood beside his buggy, with his chest heaving, opened his mouth as Houston appeared ahead of Games. 'Did what you said . . . followed him,' he panted.

'Where to?' Houston asked.

'Direction of Glim Savotta's place. Unless he's

going on somewhere.'

'No, that's about where he's headed. And it figures,' Houston nodded with satisfaction as he turned to Games. 'I reckon there's two of them storming their own puncheons right about now, Sheriff. Whatever they took from the bank, they'll be splitting it right down the middle.'

'So, you'll be accompanyin' me to the shindig?' Games asked.

Houston grinned his acceptance. 'Just try and stop me,' he said.

'We should have someone else to ride along . . . do the drivin'. This peg of mine ain't exactly mended. It'll slow me up some.'

'How about deputising Mr Land?' Houston suggested. 'He's here and fascinated by front-line action.'

Ten minutes later, and after a brief swearing-in procedure, Myron Games was being driven out of town by the thrilled, albeit nervous Orville Land. From the sidewalk, Doc Milford puffed his cheeks in frustration at the recklessness of Games. Bullhead's sheriff wasn't in shape, but he was raising a commanding hand as Houston's mare cantered alongside his buggy.

14

They reached rough, home pasture at dusk. A light glowed dully from a window in the ramshackle ranch-house. Beyond the corral there was a saddled horse tethered to a lone cottonwood and Houston called a halt.

'They'll not be waiting for us, but we'll walk from here,' he directed. 'The way I see it, Mr Land, there's nothing daring or heroic about this encounter. You might want to bear that in mind. Levitch is the son-of-a-bitch who attempted to back-shoot me. To that I don't take too kindly and that's why I'm here. For the sheriff, I'm guessing it's a matter of being deceived first ... bringing criminals to book, second. We'll just have to see how it pans out.'

'That's enough goddamn explanation,' Games responded. 'My leg's stove-up, but everythin' else is workin'. Let's get on with it.'

'No need to hurry,' Houston said. 'We know

where they are, and the darkness can be our friend.'

The three men advanced slowly, and Games was at no disadvantage. By the time they had cautiously reached the near side of the corral, it was almost full dark.

One side window hung open, and in response to a wave and pointed arm from Houston, Games stood alongside a hand pump. The barrel of his big Colt shotgun was aimed belly high on the ranch-house door. Orville Land stayed close behind Houston as they moved round towards the window.

Houston indicated that Land shouldn't move, just listen and watch. Then he ducked low, moved to the other side of the window, stood with his back close to the chinked wall. Up close, they could both now hear the eager, forceful voices of Levitch and Fats Denvy.

'You didn't drop him at the creek,' Denvy was saying. 'He was alive and kickin'. A bear with a sore head, who got Carrick off that godforsaken ground an' back on the trail. Hell, Dod, if Glim an' Jack had lived, they could've told him everythin' ... a dyin' man's words, an' all that.'

'Well they didn't to both, so quit worryin',' Levitch growled. 'An' that means *mas dinero* for you an' me.'

'Should be *mucho mas dinero* for me,' Denvy chuckled. 'None of this would have been possible without my slumber tablets. You wanted a fall guy

. . . I gave you one. You didn't even have to bend the barrel of your own gun.'

'An' you'd have been in for only a quarter of this,' Levitch countered. 'When Glim an' Jack died we profited. Now, there's more'n plenty for the two o' us.'

'I was only raggin' you, Dod,' Denvy laughed again. 'The way I'm fixed right now, a share of anythin's one hell of a lot.'

Houston stood and drew his .44 Navy Colt. In the light from a single oil lamp he could see through the ranch's narrow pantry to where Levitch and Denvy sat cater-corner at a plain table. A few bundles of bank notes and bags of coin stood beside a half-empty bottle of corn whiskey. When Houston appeared as a deeply-dark shape in the window, Levitch looked up and gasped in shock.

'He's here,' he rasped. 'Houston. He's standin' outside the goddamn window.'

'Yeah, the bear with a sore head,' Houston responded. He swung his left hand at the window frame, pushed it fully open in one fast movement.

Of the two men inside, Dod Levitch was the first to act. He swept the whiskey bottle from the table, across the room to smash against the outer wall adjacent to the window near where Houston stood.

Levitch drew his gun as he rose from the table, but Houston already had the advantage. Fats Denvy was momentarily shaken. It gave Houston time to make a decision, and he fired as Levitch backed towards the front door. Now Denvy fired, but his shot was wide, and Houston simply flinched as the bullet smacked into the side wall. Another bullet kicked splinters from the window frame, but Houston steadied himself to fire a second shot. Colts roared in angry unison, and Houston's bullet punched high into Denvy's chest. It sent the man staggering to the far wall, sliding fatally to the floor.

'Get down . . . stay out front,' Houston snapped as Land attempted to look through the window. The agitated hotel owner dropped down immediately, hunkered and patted his pockets as though seeking a weapon. Then he gulped, closed his eyes to take on the clamour, the powder flashes, the overpowering tang of burnt cordite.

Back inside, Houston seemed to be holding his fire. Through the low light he watched with a near-detached interest as Levitch reached the front door, listened with a tight, icy smile as the deputy started his desperate claim.

'I know you're out there, Myron,' the deputy sheriff started. 'The bounty man caught me an' I'm bleedin' bad. I'm not goin' anywhere. Don't shoot,' he appealed.

By the pump, Games took a single step forward. 'You're goin' somewhere all right, you treacherous scum,' he responded furiously. 'Get your rotten carcass out here.'

'Sheriff, I'm coming around. Hold your barrel high,' Houston called out. He waited a moment, stepped around the corner of the cabin as first Levitch's Colt, then Game's shotgun exploded.

Levitch was down, sprawled in a heap atop and across the narrow steps. He had dropped his Colt and was writhing in anguish, bleeding from severe wounds to the whole of his right leg.

'You been hurt?' Houston asked the sheriff.

'No, not in that way . . . not from bullets. He didn't give me a choice. But I got a hankerin' to take him back alive. Somethin' for the town to see an' chew over.'

'The other one caught a bullet too high to live,' Houston said. 'Careful how you write this, Mr Land,' he then advised. 'We don't want any of your book-reading folk to think we're all natural, cold-hearted killers.'

Allowing his excitement to overcome his fear, Orville Land had continued to tag along close behind Houston. 'I reckon this one could make a story in its own right,' he replied, staring into the night as though addressing potential readers.

'Where'd you reckon the cash is?' Games asked.

'Inside, on the table.'

'I'll take care of it,' Games decided. 'You an' Orville can get Levitch up an' onto his mount. Make sure he's safely tethered. In the darkness, we don't want him topplin' off.'

'If we don't do something about his bleeding, you know he'll die before he leaves the saddle?'

'Yeah, what a gift,' Games answered, taking a step

towards the cabin and the stolen bank money. 'I'll send out the Post brothers to bring in Denvy's body.'

They took Levitch back to town, along with the recovered cash. During the journey, and mostly for the benefit of Orville Land, Houston gave an end-to-end account of the situation. He repeated the significant facts again when he paid a late visit to Cottonwood Walk and Agnes Jarrow. The lady listened attentively, offering little comment until he had finished.

'I'm not sure it's the right word, but I am very grateful,' she murmured. 'No matter the contrary evidence, I just couldn't believe the boy was guilty. Call me soft-hearted, if you like.'

'There's probably been a few men and women who've thought like that before and to their cost. I prefer the facts . . . the reality.'

'I think you're meaning the bodies of the bad men, Mr Houston. Well, whatever, it's over now and he's in the clear. And so you'll be travelling on?' she said.

'Yes, ma'am. But first I've got to return Billy's sister, Mimsy. Then there's one or two items to pick up from Orville Land.'

'The money I offered you, it seems small compensation for all your trouble. You've risked your life.'

'That was down to me . . . mostly,' Houston conceded. 'But since accepting your offer, I have thought of a better use.'

'Really? What's that?'

'The Carricks. Make it a loan from the bank. It's somehow fitting . . . bring a long-awaited smile to their faces. There's only so much two or three men can do with picks and shovels. No wonder they've nothing to show. I reckon the money will be well invested and you'll even get repaid. A sort of exclusive grubstake. How can you refuse?'

'How indeed, Mr Houston. I'll see to it.'

Leaving the Jarrow house, Houston walked slowly along the main street. The night air was almost as stifling as it had been during the heat of the day. But soon he would be riding north towards Idaho and Yellowstone Lake.

There was a printed circular on Myron Games' desk. A notice that, for anyone interested, good money could be earned in North Montana. It was for the capture and return of Canadian border jumpers.

Houston grinned contentedly, wondered how long it had taken Bullhead's sheriff to re-discover it.